# SHARK

## INFESTED WATERS

### P.K HAWKINS

SEVERED PRESS
HOBART TASMANIA

# SHARK

Copyright © 2018 by Severed Press

*WWW.SEVEREDPRESS.COM*

*ISBN: 978-1-925711-78-3*

# CHAPTER ONE

Simon didn't have an exact word to describe the smell permeating the air. The closest he could come up with instead was a color: green. The air smelled green. The trees, the miles of endless forest, the river, the lifeforms running and scampering and screeching in the trees and underbrush. Even when it wasn't actually green, it *felt* green, lush and growing and full of life.

This was the world he'd always dreamed of visiting. This was the Amazon.

He wasn't the only one who stood on the dock and stared out at the lush world around them. Not including the captain and his two crewmembers, the tourist boat that he didn't even know the name of yet would be home for the next several days to five other people. Simon hadn't had a chance to meet any of them yet, as he'd been too busy rushing out to get his first true views of the untamed jungle river. He had to assume that everyone else had the same level of interest as him. After all, this trip hadn't been cheap for him, and anything this expensive would only attract the die-hard true believers, right?

As soon as one of them, a tall man with slicked-back black hair, opened his mouth, Simon knew differently. "This is seriously what we're paying for?" the man asked.

A young woman roughly Simon's age turned to look at the man. Despite her petite stature being dwarfed by his, she shot him a feisty look that said she would be more than willing to take him on if need be, and if Simon were a bettor, he might even put his money on her.

"What did you think you were paying for?" she asked. "Casinos on the river? Roller coasters? The whole point of a trip to the Amazon is seeing the wildest that the world has to offer."

"The wildest that the world has to offer is in my bed, sweetcheeks," the guy said. Oh brother. Simon would have done something to put the asshole in his place, but he didn't have to. The little woman was more than capable of doing it for him.

"I don't think your tiny little worm can actually be considered wild," she said. She walked away from him then, but not before "accidentally" stepping on his foot. Judging from the hardcore wince he gave, she must have more force in that tiny foot than anyone gave her credit for.

The tall man turned to Simon, giving him a look that obviously meant he expected to get some sympathy for his rude treatment. "I hate bitches like that, don't you?"

Simon tended to consider himself to be the quiet, unassuming sort. He wasn't at home with confrontation. But in this moment, it felt very important to him that he unambiguously let this guy know that he wasn't on his side. Almost before he even realized what he was doing, he gave the tall man the finger and then walked away.

With the unpleasant guy out of the way for the moment, Simon could go back to appreciating where he was and how he had gotten here. The Amazon had always been his number one dream vacation, but it had never been something he believed he'd get around to. He especially thought it would be out of the question given the massive amount of student loan debt he had to pay back now that he was done with college. But his aunt had given him the trip as a graduation present, and even though she could only afford to send him during the offseason, he was extremely grateful.

Judging from the relative age of most of the other people waiting with him at the docks for their boat, Simon suspected he wasn't the only one here to celebrate graduation. In addition to the obnoxious guy and the feisty young woman who had defied him, there were three others, a guy and a girl couple, as well as another young woman who appeared to have come with the feisty one. He hadn't had a chance to truly meet any of them yet. Simon supposed he should try to introduce himself, as the six of them were all going to be on the boat together for just under a week, cruising down the Amazon River and taking in the unspoiled wilderness, yet he just couldn't force himself to make the first move. He had always been rather shy, and nothing about this situation made that any easier.

Short-and-Feisty, however, didn't seem to have the same problem. "Hi!" she said to him, shooting out a hand for him to shake. "I'm Miriam."

"Simon," he said, taking her hand. For someone so tiny, her grip was ridiculously strong. She cocked a thumb in the direction of the other young woman who had come with her. "That's Katherine."

Katherine gave him an exaggerated wave, but said nothing else. The couple, seeing that the introductions were finally happening, came over and joined them.

"I'm Lucas, and this is my girlfriend Lara," the guy said. "Pleasure to meet you all." He then paused and looked in the direction of the taller man, who was still glowering at the river some distance away. "Or almost all of you. Miriam, was Cory giving you any trouble?"

"Not any trouble I couldn't handle," Miriam said.

"His name is Cory?" Simon asked.

"That's what he said on the bus ride over here," Lucas said. "Other than that, I didn't really bother to listen to much of what he said. Most of it was just bitching and complaining, as far as I could hear."

Simon had taken a bus from the city to here as well. It had been a small, overcrowded affair where nonetheless very few people had gotten off in this vicinity. From the stop, he'd had to hitch a ride in the back of a truck to get here. None of the others currently waiting here had been with him for any of that, so he had to wonder if there had been a way to get here that hadn't smelled like chicken and pigs.

His Aunt Annie may have paid for him to come here, but she sure hadn't been able to pay much.

Simon had to assume that most of the others were here, at this off time in the season and taking less than reliable means to get here, for the same reason. Apparently, though, they'd gotten here by different means than him.

"Did you have a bus that brought you all the way here?" Simon asked.

"No, we had to take a smaller shuttle," Miriam said. "Thankfully. Katherine here was convinced we would have to ride the rest of the way in the back of a livestock hauler, but I told her that couldn't possibly be the correct way."

Simon kept his mouth shut and tried not to blush.

Miriam, however, seemed to realize that she'd said something to make him uncomfortable. She remedied the situation by changing the subject. "Where are you from, Simon?"

"Nebraska," he said. Normally, that was something he felt self-conscious about, coming from a state that many considered to be middle-of-nowhere. But he thought he had detected just the hint of a mid-west accent in one of the other tourists, so maybe he wouldn't feel so out of his element here.

"I'm from Iowa," Lara said, confirming his theory, "although I've been living in San Diego for the last couple of years."

"And I'm San Diego born and raised," Lucas said as he affectionately kissed the top of Lara's head.

Miriam and Katherine looked like they were about to chime in with their own places of origin, but before they could, they were interrupted by a whistle from Cory back over at the dock.

"Hey, assuming the rest of you are going to be stuck on this shitty trip with me, you might want to look alive," he called. "It looks like our ride and home for the next few days is here. And it's exactly as terrible as I expected it to be."

Oh lordy, Simon wasn't looking forward to dealing with that attitude for the rest of the trip. But when he turned and looked at the boat they would be taking, he honestly had to agree with Cory. This was definitely the conveyance of tourists who couldn't afford to see the Amazon during peak times of the year with respectable tour agencies controlling it.

*Damn, Aunt Annie,* Simon thought. *I love you so much for this trip, but next time, please check the brochure a bit closer.*

There was a name stenciled on the side of the boat, but it was so chipped and faded that Simon couldn't even tell if the name was in Spanish, English, or Portuguese. If everything about the environment around them said "green," then everything about this boat said "brown," even the parts that were supposed to have color. And it wasn't a rich brown, either. It was the washed-out brown of mud and excrement and rotted leaves left to bake in the sun. The thing had obviously been around for a very long time, and Simon honestly wasn't sure how the rickety thing managed to stay afloat. About the only positive thing that could be said in its favor was that at least it was large enough for the small group of tourists to live there for several days like they were supposed to. The question then became whether or not they would even want to.

As much as everyone else looked like they wanted to defy Cory's snide statement, none of them said anything in the boat's defense. Most of them looked downright shocked at the sad state of their home for this trip, and Simon had to assume that, like him, they hadn't been the ones to arrange the specifics of their trip.

"Please tell me this is some kind of joke," Lucas said.

The boat slowed as it got to the dock, and the two deckhands stepped out to tie it off. Simon didn't know a lot about sailing, but he didn't think the knots they were using were of the best quality or workmanship. Behind these two, a third man came out of the cabin, looked around confused for a minute, then saw the tourists waiting for the boat and waved at them. While the two deckhands appeared to be locals, the man in the captain's hat had a light complexion and features that vaguely marked him as being of some kind of Eastern European stock.

"Welcome!" he bellowed at him. His thick Russian accent confirmed which part of the world he hailed from. "You must be my guests for the week! Welcome, welcome! Come aboard and join me!"

Simon looked discerningly at the boat and captain, then at the other tourists, then again at the lush world surrounding them. So then, this was to be his dream Amazon vacation. Already he could see how it would leave a little something to be desired, but at the same time, he hadn't expected five days in the rainforest and along the Amazon River to be a pleasure cruise. He'd wanted to see the real river, not some overly touristy version of it, and that apparently was what he was going to get. He would take the bad, as long as it brought all the amazing world of his dreams along with it.

After all, despite the company, despite the janky nature of the boat and the strange-acting captain, this was something people did a lot. What was the worst that could happen?

Simon grabbed his backpack with his belongings and was the first to approach the boat. Following his lead, the remaining tourists took up their own possessions and boarded along with him. None of them took notice of the shifting change in the wind, or the dark clouds that had just popped up far away on the horizon. And none of them, not a single one, thought for even one second that they might not leave the Amazon River alive.

# CHAPTER TWO

Simon would have expected the captain of the boat to introduce himself, or at least give some kind of prepared speech, but much to his surprise, the captain promptly disappeared from sight while his two deckhands loaded up some supplies that had been left on the dock. The tourists were left to mull about on the deck, each of them unsure of what they were supposed to do next.

"Is it just me, or does this seem a bit disorganized?" Lara asked to none of them in particular.

"I told you," Cory loudly said to her from where he was standing on the far side of the deck. "This whole thing is a shitshow."

And just like that, everyone was concentrating less on the peculiar circumstances surrounding their boat and its captain and more on exactly how much they disliked Cory again. "What is even your problem?" Katherine asked him. The other tourists, whether they meant to or not, started to converge around him. "You obviously don't want to be here even a little bit, so why not just turn around and go home to let the rest of us actually enjoy this?"

"You actually think any of you are going to enjoy this?" Cory asked. He kicked the wood of the boat's railing to emphasize his point. The wood shuddered more than safety regulations would have deemed acceptable anywhere else in the world.

Simon tried to hide how much the display disturbed him. He really was getting a little concerned about the safety of the boat, but he didn't want to let Cory know that he thought the tall man was even a little right. Something told Simon that any such sign or display would turn Cory into an even more insufferable know-it-all.

"Um, excuse me?" Lucas asked one of the deckhands. "Could one of you tell us what we're supposed to do with our stuff? Are we all supposed to go to some kind of bunks or something?"

The deckhand said something in what Simon assumed was Portuguese. He also made a few gestures that Simon believed were supposed to be directions, but before anyone could ask the man to elaborate, he was off again to do whatever it was he was supposed to do on the boat.

Katherine gave everyone else a look that was both confused and annoyed. "So I guess maybe we should go find our own bunks? Or rooms? Or whatever the hell it is we're supposed to have. Does anyone here even know for sure?"

A quick, non-verbal survey resulted in everyone shaking their heads.

"So, is there anyone that was aware this was what we were getting when they signed up for the trip?" Simon asked.

"No," Miriam said. "Were you?"

"This trip was a graduation gift," Simon said. "I was too excited to even be going to pay too much attention to the details. I just figured I shouldn't look a gift-horse in the mouth."

"Uh, yeah," Miriam said. "And I've kinda gotta admit something: Katherine and I signed up for this trip while we were drunk. We weren't exactly paying attention to the details, either."

"Lucas bought this trip for me as a present," Lara said. In

response, her boyfriend wrapped his arms around her from behind. "Neither of us has a lot of money, so we just took whatever we could get."

They all turned to look at Cory to see if he would join in the conversation, but he was too busy sullenly sulking around the front of the boat to pay any attention to what they were saying.

Right, Simon thought. So none of them had been completely aware of what they were getting into with this trip. But he still wasn't going to let the less-than-stellar details get him down. So the trip might be a bit on the rough side. Again, this was the Amazon, one of the wildest places still left on Earth. It would have been disingenuous to expect a cruise ship or anything like that. At the very least, they were on a boat that looked like it had done its rounds up and down the massive river. The captain had to know what he was doing.

As if on cue, the captain came back out onto the deck. Before even acknowledging any of them, he went to the edge of the deck, positioned himself so that his crotch was just over the railing, and started to pull down the zipper of his pants.

"Um, excuse me?" Miriam said to him.

The captain startled, and Simon realized that he hadn't been ignoring them after all. He simply hadn't been bothered to notice their existence.

"What are you doing here?" the captain asked, whirling to see them with his fly still halfway down on his pants. His thick accent might not have been Russian after all, but Simon couldn't place exactly where it was from. "Get off my boat, or I'll call security."

Simon and several of the others looked around just to make sure there was no security of any kind.

"Um, we're supposed to be here?" Lucas said to him. "We're your customers. We all paid to do your five-day trip on the

Amazon."

The captain stared at them all through heavily lidded eyes before he blinked. "Oh. Oh! Yes, um. Welcome. Aboard? Yes, aboard. That thing."

And then he turned and started back to the cabin as though he was planning on further ignoring them.

"Wait!" Miriam called after him. "Aren't you supposed to give us some kind of orientation or something? Tell us what to expect on the trip? Or even at least let us know where we should be putting our stuff?"

The captain looked surprised that anyone had deigned to speak to him like that. He turned to one of his deckhands and spoke to him in hurried, confused Portuguese, leaving the young tourists to speak amongst themselves again for several minutes.

"Miriam, have you noticed anything off about our intrepid captain?" Katherine asked her friend.

"What, do you mean besides the fact that he looks like he intentionally smears mud in his beard to get it to stick out in all those directions?"

Now that the two of them were talking about it, Simon also realized that something seemed off about their captain, and it wasn't just his bizarre behavior. The way he moved, Simon would have thought they were already out on the river instead of docked. He swayed just a little this way and that, like he was compensating for the rocking of waves that only he could feel.

As soon as it occurred to him exactly what was wrong with the captain, Simon had to wonder why he hadn't realized it sooner. But then again, maybe he could be forgiven for automatically assuming that the captain they were paying to take them through one of the wildest parts left on Earth would be responsible enough not to be drunk at the beginning of their voyage.

Cory joined the group again, and for once, the words that came out of his mouth actually added something to their conversation without making everyone want to smack him. "I recognized that smell on his breath. That's the same whiskey my uncle used to drink all the time."

"He doesn't drink it anymore?" Lara asked.

"No. He drove drunk and smashed his car into a construction crane. Killed himself instantly."

"Uh. Oh," was all Lara could say in response.

"Well shit," Lucas said. He began to gather up his luggage and looked like he was about to take it off the boat before it could leave the dock.

"What are you doing?" Lara asked him.

"Babe, what do you think I'm doing? I'm not going down the Amazon River with a drunk captain."

"But we put so much of our savings into this trip!" Lara said. "We can't just walk away from it now after we've come this far."

"Yeah, and also, do you know something that the rest of us don't regarding transportation?" Miriam asked. "Because merely getting bussed down to this point was difficult enough. The bus or vans or whatever only run down this far because they were paid to. It's not like they're going to just pop up at random again just in case there happens to be someone waiting for them at a dock in the middle of nowhere."

"There's going to be a ride waiting for us at the place where we get off the boat," Katherine said. "Other than that, you might as well walk off into the middle of the rainforest. It would get you back to a town or city faster than waiting."

"Come on. There's got to be something," Lucas said. "Whatever company set this tour up, they had to provide some way to go back if there was a problem."

"Honey, I'm the one that set up this trip for us," Lara said. "I had to, if I wanted to do it on our budget."

"And you didn't check to see if the captain might be an incompetent, raging alcoholic?"

"How the hell was I supposed to do that? He's a guy that runs his own tour boat on the Amazon. It's not like he's going to have a page for Yelp reviews."

"You see, everyone?" Cory asked. "I told you this was going to be a shitshow."

"Look, I don't think there's anything we can do about any of this," Simon said. He was a bit surprised that he had the nerve to speak up, but no one else seemed to be getting anywhere. "We're here, and we can't leave by any means other than the boat taking us to where it's eventually supposed to stop. And yeah, the captain certainly seems iffy, but it's not like this is his first time." Or at least Simon didn't think it was. He had to trust that Aunt Annie hadn't set him up with some random guy no one had ever heard of. "He's obviously done this a time or two, and despite the state of everything, he's still sailing and his boat is still floating."

"You're kidding me, right?" Cory said. "This guy has so much booze in him that I'm afraid to light a match around him."

"Well, I guess we don't really have a choice at this point," Katherine said. "We're here and we can't go back the way we came. So the best we can do is try to make the best of this. And maybe Simon's right. Maybe there's more to our captain than meets the eye. He might not be the total screw-up that he looks like."

As one, they all looked in the direction of the captain. He'd finished talking with his deckhand, and against all odds, he did suddenly seem to be lucid. The captain approached them again, and although he still wobbled, at least this time he looked like he was trying not to sway on his feet.

"I apologize," the captain said. "I got off on the wrong toe.

Toe? Foot. I mean foot. Please, take your belongings to the bunks just below deck. Once you have settled in, come back up and we'll begin the tour. Welcome to the Amazon."

It was hardly the greatest welcome speech in history, but at least it was better than what the captain had offered them earlier. The deckhand that the captain had been speaking to waved for them all to follow him, presumably down to their bunks, and Simon allowed himself a sliver of hope. This could still be his dream vacation. It might be rough, but then he hadn't expected life going through the Amazon to be easy. As long as he kept his expectations at a reasonable level, this could still be a trip he would never forget.

# CHAPTER THREE

For roughly an hour after their boat finally launched from the dock, Simon managed to convince himself that the trip would actually be something enjoyable. The captain, while still unsteady on his feet and smelling faintly of multiple variations of alcohol, was much more personable than he'd initially come off, and he chatted amiably with several of the tourists as his vessel started its way down one of the longest rivers in the world. He even started to show the hints of being an accomplished tour guide, giving a few pieces of information about the Amazon that managed to be of marginal interest to Simon's fellow passengers. Simon, however, had studied the Amazon River and rainforest enough that the captain's tidbits seemed to him to be just rehashes of basic knowledge.

Of course, Simon had to remind himself that not everyone, even if they were on this trip, was going to be as educated about the region as he was. Simon's fascination with the Amazon had begun at an early age thanks to a music teacher in grade school who could only be called a tree-hugging hippy, and who, rather than being offended by that phrase, would have embraced it. The teacher had decorated her classroom with all manner of pictures of endangered animal and plant life, with most of it belonging to the rainforest regions. Simon had loved that teacher, and had been suitably devastated when she had died from cancer before he had finished his elementary school career. Even gone, though, her teachings had continued to influence him, moving him all the rest of the way through school and leading him eventually to this place and his dream of visiting coming true.

Despite his knowledge, though, Simon kept his mouth shut whenever anyone else, including the captain himself, said anything that was either suspect or flat-out wrong regarding the Amazon. He had no particular need to embarrass others or try to elevate himself. This trip wasn't about making himself feel superior at the expense of others. So, instead, he was content with listening, correcting any falsehoods he heard in his mind while otherwise simply enjoying himself.

As the hours moved on, however, Simon started to realize that the trip wasn't going to be completely smooth the whole way. In particular, he didn't think the weather was going to stay as pleasant as it had been when they'd all boarded the boat. He'd known in advance that he would be heading down here at the beginning of the rainy season (and that was likely another reason his aunt had been able to get the trip for so cheap), so it didn't surprise him when things took a turn. However, as he'd never experienced the weather down here himself before, he was unprepared for the speed with which it all changed.

While the sky had been an impossible blue earlier in the day, it was now gray and harsh, with the wind starting to come in over the river in unsettling bursts. The water rippled, and the many examples of visible life beneath the surface looked unusually active, like the weather was a portent of something for them to come. In addition to knowing about the rainy season, he also knew intellectually that "rainy" had a different meaning here on the Amazon River than it did back home. It was called a rainforest for a reason. There was no such thing as a light shower here.

While Simon had been fascinated by the changing of the weather, Miriam and Katherine had apparently been busy actually preparing for it. When Simon finally turned away from the approaching storm clouds that had mesmerized him, he saw that the two young women had gone down below deck and pulled out a number of ponchos. The captain himself was no longer anywhere to be found, as he was likely in the cabin prepping for the inclement weather, leaving the tourists to once again take matters of their own safety and comfort into their own hands. Simon nodded in thanks as he took a poncho from Miriam, then looked around to see that the three of them were the only ones still on deck.

"Where'd everyone else go?" Simon asked.

"While you were acting like you were hypnotized by the clouds, Lucas and Lara went down to the bunks. Judging from the way they were pawing and crawling all over each other, I'm thinking you might not want to go down there for a bit unless you want to get an X-rated eyeful," Miriam said. She slipped her own poncho over her head, prompting Simon to do the same. "As for the Jackass, I don't know where he went and I don't care."

Simon didn't have to ask who she meant by "the Jackass."

Katherine pulled up the hood on her poncho and pulled it tight around her face. "We're not going to stay out here, are we? Whatever's coming, it doesn't exactly look pleasant."

"Katherine, perhaps you missed the part where we're down here to see the world's largest rainforest," Miriam said to her. "As in, there's going to be rain."

"But there's not going to be a lot, right?"

"Let me repeat: raaaaaaaainforest."

Simon couldn't help but be amused by this exchange. "What brings you two here for this trip, anyway? Other than having too much to drink."

"It's part of an independent study we set up for our college classes," Miriam said.

"No, it's part of an independent study that Miriam set up," Katherine corrected. "She just wanted an excuse to take some time off from school, and we'd already done our drunk booking, so she bullshitted our advisors into believing this trip would somehow give us experience we couldn't get back home."

"What is it you two are studying?" Simon asked.

Miriam grinned despite the distant thunder rumbling through the air and promising very interesting things to come. "Katherine's doing veterinary science."

Simon paused and thought about that. "Well, I guess I could see how that's connected if I stretched my mind."

Miriam's grin got even bigger. "And I'm business management."

This time, Simon's pause was longer. "That's a connection that's a little bit harder to grasp."

Miriam shrugged, her oversized poncho making an abnormally large crinkly noise on her small frame. "Business management is so useless that even the people who teach it don't have a good idea of what it's for, so you can convince them that pretty much *everything* is related to business." Her words, her smile, and the way the poncho hung on her brought Simon to mind of some kind of fairy-tale trickster imp, and he found himself with the slight pang of a crush.

He didn't have any time to dwell on that feeling though, as that was the moment the sky finally opened up and dropped on them. Simon made sure his hood was up just in time to prevent a thorough soaking of his head. While he was entirely unsurprised by the sudden ferocity of the downpour, Katherine squealed in dismay.

"Miriam, we're going inside or something now, right?"

Miriam looked for a moment like she was going to follow her friend, but once she saw that Simon was making no effort to get to someplace drier, she paused. "Aren't you coming in, too?"

Simon thought about it, then shook his head. "I came here to experience the Amazon. This is part of it. You two go on in. I'll be fine."

But rather than seek shelter, Miriam waved her friend off. "You go in. I'll join you soon."

Katherine looked at her like the rain had already drowned a few of Miriam's brain cells, but she didn't stick around long enough to argue about it. Once she was gone and disappeared into the main cabin, Miriam turned and looked at Simon with unmistakable curiosity. "You really don't care about getting wet just because it's all part of where we are?"

"Coming to the Amazon has been a dream of mine since I was a kid. If I didn't want to get wet, I could have stayed home and just read all the books I have about it."

"What's so great about the Amazon that you're so obsessed about it?" From anyone else, the question might have sounded vaguely insulting. But the way Miriam said it, Simon got the impression that she found him to be some kind of strange and interesting specimen that had caught her curiosity.

"It's some of the highest density of life in the world," Simon said. "Even with so many species dying and going extinct for various reasons, there's things here you would never expect. Frogs, birds, snakes, lizards, sloths, sharks, dolphins…"

"Wait, dolphins? There's no dolphins in the Amazon. And I'm pretty sure there's no sharks, either. Maybe like, piranhas or something, but…"

"Oh no, there are definitely both," Simon said. "Not only are there dolphins in the Amazon River, but they're pink."

"Shut up," Miriam said with a laugh. "Now I know you're

lying."

"I swear I'm not. And the sharks that live in the Amazon River are bull sharks. They swim up the river from the sea, but because of that, you only ever really see them in the Brazilian portion of the river. It would be highly unlikely that we would see any sharks like that on the portion of the river that we're going down."

"Uh-huh," Miriam said. "Sounds to me like a good excuse to keep me from calling you out on bullshitting me."

"I swear it's true. Look it up when we get home."

There was a moment of awkward silence between them where Simon finally realized how ridiculous it was for them to be having this conversation outside in the middle of a rain storm. Miriam seemed to realize it too, and yet she still seemed hesitant to leave him. Finally, she said, "You're really going to just sit out here grinning like an idiot in the rain?"

"Just for a bit. I'll go back in where it's dry shortly. From what I've seen so far, there's not a lot of places we can go other than the main cabin and the bunks below deck. The captain is probably in the cabin trying to sneak sips of tequila, and I don't think any of us want to walk in on Lucas and Lara right now."

"There's got to be somewhere else we could go," Miriam said. "Somewhere we could talk without getting drenched."

Only then did it occur to Simon that she might be trying to flirt with him. He wasn't usually the type of person that women wanted to flirt with, and he was perfectly okay with that, but Miriam didn't seem like a typical girl either. Maybe it would be worth his while to go with her and try to find some place relatively private, if that was even possible on such a small boat.

But, truth be told, he didn't want to leave the deck just yet. He was actually enjoying the start of his dream trip, drenching and all. "If it's all the same to you, I think I'll just stay here."

He watched Miriam out of the corner of his eye and saw the way she waffled. Whether she was actively trying to flirt with him or else she was just intrigued by him, she obviously wanted to stick around. At the same time, though, Miriam was also not quite as keen to be standing out in a storm as he was.

"If it affects your decision any," Simon said, "this is probably not going to be the only time you're going to be wet on this trip."

It was only after the words came out of his mouth that he realized what he said could be taken as a double entendre. Before he could stammer out an apology, though, Miriam laughed and took up a more permanent position next to him at the boat's railing.

"No, I suppose it won't," Miriam said. Her tone suggested that she had definitely picked up on the possible double meaning, and that she might actually be interested in making the second meaning of his phrase a reality.

Unfortunately for them both, neither of them got any further chance to explore the growing sexual tension between them. Because within minutes, their little trip was about to become a fight for survival.

# CHAPTER FOUR

The sky had already been dark from the cloud cover, but as night fell, the visibility dropped to practically nothing, as far as Simon could see. For a few minutes, this didn't concern him, as he was too distracted by the growing flirtations between him and Miriam. She had to be the one to point out what he should have already seen.

"Uh, hey, Simon?" she asked. "Is it just me, or is the boat going a little too fast for how dark it is out here?"

She was absolutely right. Not only had the boat not reduced its speed at all—in fact, he couldn't be sure, but it might be going faster than earlier—but there were no lights on anywhere near the front of the boat to show potential obstacles that might be in their way. If the boat had been going straight down the middle of the broad river, he might not have found this so alarming. However, the last time he had been able to clearly see, the boat had been rather close to the south shore, where there were a number of trees and roots visible. Those might not have been a problem during the drier season, but as the depth of the river speedily rose with the rain, the trees would actually appear to be growing from the river itself, making them a notable hazard even to someone like Simon who had very little knowledge of boatcraft.

"What the hell?" Simon muttered under his breath. He turned and went in the direction of the cabin. At the door, he saw that the captain, Katherine, and Cory were all inside, with the two men deep into a heated argument. Just judging from the first few things Simon heard out of Cory's mouth, this would be the first time since they'd met this afternoon that the two of them would be in total agreement.

"If you're going to be this drunk, then you either you need one of your people to take over for you or else stop the boat entirely," Cory said.

The captain glared at him, and it almost seemed to Simon that the captain was so drunk that, somehow despite all reason and logic, even his glare seemed slurred by the drink. Amazingly, though, his words came out of his mouth just fine. "I've been captaining on this river since before you were a stain in your father's underwear, boy. I know what I'm doing, and I say we're fine."

The captain paused for a moment as though thinking, then went to the controls and fiddled with them. Simon immediately felt a lurch beneath his feet as the boat sped up even more.

"What the hell are you—?" Before Simon could finish his sentence, Cory went for the controls himself. The captain blocked the way, trying to hit Cory in the process, but couldn't land the blow even from such a close distance. Katherine screamed and tried to get out of their way, but the cabin was small enough that all she managed to do was get in their way further. As the two of them scuffled, Cory shoved the captain, who fell back onto the controls. There was an audible snap, and once Simon could see the controls again, several of the levers were either bent or broken.

"You idiot!" both Simon and Miriam screamed at the same time. The boat lurched again, the busted controls apparently telling it that it still hadn't been going fast enough.

The captain stood dumbfounded while Cory tried to find a

way to slow the boat down. Simon, meanwhile, went back out onto the deck. "Someone turn on the lights!" he yelled through the rain and back into the cabin. "We need to see if we're about to run into anything!"

The captain continued to loudly protest while someone else found the controls for the front lights. As they snapped on, Lucas and Lara came back out on the deck, as well as the two deckhands. While the deckhands looked prepared for the weather, neither of the lovers were wearing ponchos. In fact, Lucas's fly wasn't even zipped. Apparently, they hadn't been completely finished with each other before the boat had started doing its NASCAR impression. "What's going on?" Lara asked. Simon could barely hear her over the sounds of the storm and the rain pelting the water all around them, not that he would have had a chance to answer the question anyway.

He was too preoccupied with what he could now see in the flood of light ahead of the boat. There was a row of trees there and many visible, extremely pointy roots visible just below the water. And the boat was headed right for them.

Simon screamed out to the others. "Everyone brace yourselves!"

Most of the passengers didn't seem to hear him. They also didn't need to, as most of the others on the deck had already seen the same thing as him and were already clinging for dear life to anything that was bolted down. Simon closed his eyes just before impact, so he didn't see the exact moment the boat hit the first tree, but he could feel multiple hits as the roots punched a staccato series of holes in the side. His brain briefly flashed back to the moment earlier when Cory had kicked the wood at the side of the boat and it had an alarming amount of give. If that was the poor shape of the boat above the water, then it wasn't so surprising that something as simple as tree roots could do massive damage to the vessel below the water line. The entire boat shook violently and lurched, throwing one of the two deckhands from his place and sending him screaming into the water. Simon thought he heard the splash, but honestly, he couldn't be sure over the screaming of the others and the horrific rending of wood and metal. There was a sudden, disorienting feeling like vertigo, and Simon realized that the boat was no longer chugging along straight ahead. It had deflected off the trees and was now doing a graceless pirouette back in the direction of the center of the river. They might not have been so close to the hazards anymore, but with the holes that had to now be filling with water, it wasn't like they wanted to be farther away from the shore anymore. If the boat sank while they were out in the middle of the river, there would be far more likelihood of them all drowning than if it went down where they had first been.

"Abandon ship!" Simon screamed.

"Wait, what?" Miriam called back. Simon hadn't even realized she was back on the deck again, nor did he waste any time trying to turn and find her. Instead, he immediately began searching the deck for anything that resembled a life preserver. There was nothing that he could see. Apparently, the captain was just as lax with safety regulations as he was with his sobriety.

"We can't just jump off the boat," Lucas called out. The remaining deckhand, however, whether he understood what Simon said or not, was of the same mind as Simon. He ran and tried to make a vault over the railing into the water, but the boat juked at the last second, causing his feet to tangle on the edge of the boat and sending him flying gracelessly head over heels into the water.

"We've got to get off while we're still close to the shore," Simon called, but he was no longer sure which direction the nearest shore was even in. Beneath his feet, the deck had started to tilt at an alarming angle, and with the slickness of the boards, he was finding it suddenly difficult to keep his balance.

"He's right!" Miriam called out. "We have to get off now!"

"I'm not sure if I can swim that far," Katherine said.

"We'll all jump off at the same time," Simon said. "Maybe we'll be able to help each other to shore."

Somewhere else on the boat, there was a high-pitched scream that managed to pierce the roar of the rain. It had to have come from the captain, but none of them had time to try finding him. The boat violently hit something else below the surface, almost as though it were trying to tell them that, if they wanted to escape, this was their final warning.

They had all run up to the railing by now, and they were on the side that had dipped lowest in the water. When Simon looked over the side, he found that the river, seemingly alive and writhing as millions of raindrops aggravated the surface, was only about a foot below where they all stood. It wouldn't be a huge jump, but he was sure the water would be a cold shock to all their systems the instant they were submerged in it. Suddenly, any bravado and bravery that Simon had felt moments earlier was gone. His fun vacation of a lifetime was already becoming a total nightmare, and something told him that, even if he didn't drown here, the nightmare was going to continue.

Whether it was because she noticed his hesitation or because she needed a little courage herself, Miriam slipped her hand into Simon's. Her hand was clammy from the rain, but stronger than her small frame would have implied. Simon looked at her with appreciation, which she acknowledged with a nod. On her other side, she was holding hands with Katherine, who looked positively beside herself with terror. Some of that water streaming down her face, Simon was sure, would be tears rather than rainwater. Lucas and Lara, further down the railing, were also holding hands. Cory, to Simon's complete lack of surprise, held no one's hand at all and actually looked a little disgusted that the rest of them needed any reassurance.

"We'll all jump over on three," Simon called out. Indeed, the angle of the boat was such that they probably wouldn't have even been able to stand on it without sliding into the railing for much longer than a few seconds anyway. He wasn't sure if this part of the river was deep enough for the entire boat to get submerged, but even if it just went down another few feet, there wasn't going to be any place for them to properly stand for much longer.

Before Simon could even start calling numbers, however, something below deck blew up. Later, Simon would suppose that it had to be something with the engine, and that maybe whatever had caused the catastrophic engine conflagration was also the reason the captain had screamed seconds earlier. In the moment, however, there was no time for such thoughts. All there was instead was a sudden push from beneath them, and then all six tourists were flying through the rainy night, heading for the chilly waters of the Amazon.

# CHAPTER FIVE

Simon had thought he had prepared himself for the shock of hitting the river, given that he'd already been standing out in the rain from the moment it had started. He was wrong.

The Amazon River was cold, colder than anything so close to the Equator had any right to be. He had thought to keep his mouth closed as he went under, but the sudden change of temperature made him yelp inadvertently, instantly giving him a mouthful and literally taking his breath away. Even though the drop was relatively short, he found himself going deeper into the water than expected, and he had to struggle for several precious seconds to get his head back above the surface for a precious gulp of air. Even once he did, the shock and confusion of the situation prevented him from immediately trying to get to safety. Then he realized that, somewhere in the chaos, he had let go of Miriam's hand. He couldn't immediately see where she had gone, nor did he have the time to try finding her. They had all been facing the same direction, so hopefully, they all ended up in the same place.

And also, hopefully, that same place wasn't at the bottom of the river as rotting corpses feeding the fish.

Simon started swimming, going directly ahead, but found quickly that his precautions against the rain earlier were hampering him now. The poncho wrapped around his body both made it hard for him to do the correct swimming motions, as well as created drag. The swiftly moving waters of the river grabbed onto his plastic garment and threatened to pull him off in some far unknown direction. Although he knew he might miss it later, Simon struggled out of the poncho and let it float away, freeing him up to save himself in the moment. After all, it wasn't like he needed it to keep him from getting wet anymore.

Several times, waves lapped over his head, causing him to sputter. He tried to look around and get some idea of his environment, but the darkness and the storm kept him from seeing anything other than water. His body tired quickly and his lungs burned with the need to cough out the river water he had inhaled, but he kept going straight ahead, hoping that he hadn't gotten too turned around and was heading to the shore rather than deeper into the river. His limbs started to give out, and several times he started to sink. The second time, however, his knees only went down a short distance before coming in contact with the silt at the bottom of the river. With one final burst of energy, he pulled himself forward and found himself crawling up onto land.

When he finally finished coughing up lungfuls of water, Simon pushed himself into a sitting position and took stock of who and what had ended up on the small muddy patch of dirt with him. Several bits of flotsam from the boat had washed up next to him, some of which had Miriam still clinging to it as an impromptu lifesaver a few feet out yet from the shore. There were other noticeable pieces of the boat floating about, but for the moment, he couldn't see the exact location of the wreck through the rain and darkness. Several splashes nearby told him that there were still others swimming for his patch of land.

Speaking of the land, just where the hell exactly was he? The darkness of the rain clouds had made it hard enough to see before, but it was even worse now that it was full night, and

Simon had trouble getting much of a read on the place where he had come ashore. He couldn't even be sure if he'd washed up on the north or the south bank of the Amazon. He'd been completely turned around and lost all sense of direction during the wreck. He supposed that wasn't the most important thing to know at this exact moment, considering there were still people in the water and supplies they would need to find if they were going to do anything about their situation, but something about this still made Simon uneasy.

He didn't have time to dwell on that, though, as the first of his companions from the boat came sputtering to the edge of his patch of land. Miriam stumbled up onto land first, with Katherine shortly behind her. Miriam had ditched her poncho as well, but Katherine had somehow managed to make it the whole way with the heavy garment still on. Katherine sobbed as she pulled herself up through the mud at the bank, and Miriam immediately went to her side to help her.

"Where—?" Simon's question was interrupted as he went into a coughing fit, spitting up more water and a not insignificant amount of mucus onto the ground by his feet. Once he caught his breath, he tried again. "Where are the others? Did either of you see them?"

There were further splashing noises somewhere else nearby in the darkness, followed by Cory croaking out, "I'm here."

Simon followed his voice until he was close enough to see him. "Have you seen Lucas and Lara? Or either of the deckhands?"

"Do I look like I've had a chance to run around looking for anyone?" Cory asked. He punctuated this by ringing out his waterlogged shirt directly onto Simon's feet, not that it was much of an insult when his shoes were already completely soggy. Simon ignored him and started moving down the shore, looking for any sign of the others. He didn't immediately find anyone, but as he followed the area where the water met the land, he quickly realized they were not as out of danger as they had hoped. He followed the curving shore for just over a minute and a half before he found himself right back where he started. Miriam and Katherine were helping Lucas and Lara up onto land, but as soon as Miriam saw Simon coming from the opposite direction of where he had gone, she hissed in a breath.

"We're not on the north or south shore of the river, are we?" she asked.

"Nope," Simon said. "We're on an island in the middle of the river."

"You've got to be kidding me," Cory said. With anyone else, that might have been simply an exclamation of dismay. Cory, however, apparently refused to actually believe it and immediately started walking the perimeter of the island as though that was going to disprove something. While Cory did that, Simon told the others what little he had seen. They were simply on a nearly bare patch of land with nothing more than a few grasses and other unidentifiable plants trying to eke out an existence here.

As Cory came back around the other side, Lara spoke up. "Why is everyone acting like this is so terrible? We're alive, aren't we? And since we managed to swim this far, we should be able to swim to shore as well, right?"

Simon looked around at the others to see if any of them had figured out exactly how bad off they really were. Miriam didn't disappoint. "No, honey, it's not going to be that simple," Miriam said. "I'm betting that as long as the rain is going, the river isn't going to be something we want to try swimming in."

"She's right," Simon said. "Especially right now at night. The current is going to be ridiculously strong, and we can't even see exactly which direction we need to go in. We wouldn't be able to get out of here until at least the morning."

"Fine, so we do that," Lucas said.

"Except I don't think that's going to work, either," Miriam said. She was looking down at their feet, specifically the place where the water met the land. She had to be noticing the same thing Simon had been afraid of. "We might not be able to wait that long."

"What do you mean?" Lara asked.

"She means the water's rising," Simon said. "Don't forget that we got here on the Amazon at the start of the rainiest season. The river was at a lower point just hours ago, but the rain is bringing the level up, and it's not going to stop. We may be at what would be an island in the drier season, but we just so happen to be here on the days islands vanish. The river's going to keep getting deeper until the land we're on is completely underwater."

Even in the poor light, Simon could see the way several of his companions paled. "How long do we have before this island is under water?"

At this, Simon had to shrug. "That I couldn't tell you."

Miriam, however, seemed to be doing some calculations in her head. "By my best guess, if the rain keeps up at this rate, we maybe have until a little before dawn. Perhaps a little longer if the rain lets up."

"So we can't stay here," Lucas said. "Right. So let's start swimming."

"Are you deaf or just an idiot?" Cory asked. "It's already been established that trying to swim isn't going to get us anywhere if we don't even know where we're going."

Katherine had already started staring out into the darkness in search of any clue about what direction they should go, although she seemed to be doing it more out of hysterics than because she realized it was the proper thing to do. "We've got to get out of here. There has to be a way." Before anyone could say anything more to her, she stood straighter and then pointed to something out in the gloom. "There! What's that? Is that somewhere we could go?"

Everyone else joined her where she stood and tried to see whatever she'd seen. After some squinting, Simon thought he knew what she was pointing at. "I think that's the boat. Or what's left of it."

The longer they all stared, the more they all seemed to agree with him. It was definitely the boat that had gotten them all into this mess, but it was hardly recognizable as such anymore. It had to have caught on something in the river, preventing it from going farther downstream or plunging deeper into the waters. Part of the stern was still visible above the water, while a significant portion of the cabin was still visible. The irony, it appeared, was that their group would have probably been safer if they hadn't jumped off the boat at all, but had instead climbed up on the roof of the cabin. At the very least, it would have kept them out of the river for longer than this island would.

It would have been the perfect place for them to try retreating to, if not for one unfortunate fact. Simon shook his head. "It's too far upriver from us," he said. "If the waters weren't so fast right now, then maybe we could make it. But unless one of us is an Olympic swimmer, we wouldn't be able to make it." Still, it was a landmark for them to keep in mind. Simon filed it away, just in case he might figure out a way to reach it.

"What about that over there?" Miriam asked, pointing in a different direction. Now that Simon had had a chance to examine the flow of the water, he thought he could use it to determine direction. The Amazon River flowed in a generally eastern direction, after all, which meant that Miriam was pointing to the north.

"It looks like another patch of land," Cory said about her discovery. "Kind of hard to tell from here, but maybe it's bigger than what we're currently standing on."

Simon, however, didn't get a chance to think on or comment about that. He was too preoccupied with the shapes he now saw sluicing their way through the water. They were triangular and floating around them with ease. In fact, as he followed the dim shapes with his eyes, it looked like they were circling the island.

"Oh shit," Miriam said. "I can't tell color in this light. Please tell me those fins in the water are pink."

As everyone else also saw the forms swimming through the river, Simon could only shake his head. "They're the wrong shape to belong to botos."

"Botos?" Lucas asked.

"Pink Amazon River dolphins," Simon said.

"There's dolphins in the Amazon? Really?" Lara asked.

"Apparently, but it doesn't matter," Miriam said. "Because these aren't them."

"Then what are they?" Lucas asked.

"Bull sharks," Simon said. "I guess I was wrong, Miriam. I guess they can get this far up the river."

He didn't have to add that the bull sharks had had to go wherever there was food. They'd certainly found it, and now all they had to do was wait for the waters to rise enough to reach that food.

If Miriam's calculations on how long it would take for the island to vanish under the river were correct, then it seemed that all six of the survivors here would probably be inside a shark's belly by sunup.

# CHAPTER SIX

There were a lot of things the six of them needed to deal with in a short amount of time, and it was evident right away that one of them would need to act as the person in charge. Simon voiced his concern about this, only for Cory to immediately act incensed.

"No, you don't get to be the leader here," Cory said. "Out of everyone here, I definitely think I'm the one who's the most qualified, so I get to be the one who calls the shots."

Simon looked around at the others. He hadn't actually thought of himself as trying to be the leader—he was pretty sure he was the last one here capable of leading anyone, after all, and he'd hoped someone else would take up that mantle—but in terms of being qualified, literally anyone other than Cory would have worked better. And through the mud and tear-streaked masks on each of the other survivors, he could see that each and every one of them agreed with him.

On unspoken agreement, they all turned away from Cory and faced each other in a loose circle, a circle that clearly did not include the tall young man who had just proclaimed that he was in charge. Simon didn't even give Cory the respect of looking for the reaction on his face. They had far more important things to worry about just now.

"What are we going to do?" Lara asked through chattering teeth. "The captain and both of the deckhands are dead, aren't they?"

"The captain, I think, is dead for sure," Katherine said, her voice stuttering as her teeth chattered. "If he's not, then I'd kind of be afraid to see what state he's in, given the way he screamed."

"It sounded like he might have been trying to do something in the engine room that caused that explosion," Miriam said.

"But couldn't either of the deckhands still be alive?" Lucas asked.

"Maybe," Simon said. "Has anybody seen any sign of either of them?"

One by one, each of the tourists shook their heads.

"Well, if either of them is alive, they're still not here," Simon said. "They either drowned and were swept further down the river or else made it to shore. Whichever it was, we have to assume they're not going to be in any position to help us."

"So we've got to figure this out on our own," Miriam said. She looked at each of the others in turn, although her gaze seemed to linger the longest on Simon. "Maybe we should start by figuring out what we have available to use if we need it. Anything at all that could be helpful."

Unfortunately, that didn't turn out to be much of anything. None of them had been carrying any kind of survival supplies on their person at the time of the shipwreck, considering no one had expected everything to go so wrong so quickly. They did at least still have Katherine's poncho, which could be used as a blank or a rather poor shelter in a pinch. There were also the various pieces of flotsam that had washed up with them, consisting mainly of wooden pieces of the boat. Beyond that, they pretty much just had the clothes on their backs. None of them even seemed to have purses or wallets, as all of that had been with their personal items in the bunk area. Lucas did at least find a length of rope that had been used to tie down the boat, which was discovered as it bobbed in a shallow place at the edge of the island, temporarily caught in an eddy before it would have soon floated off down the river with the rest of the debris. They gathered up all these bits of detritus, along with a couple of pieces of driftwood, and piled them together at the center of their island. As far as size went, the pile was pretty pathetic.

"It might be enough to start a fire," Lucas said. "Maybe we should do that. Isn't that what you're supposed to do in situations like this?"

"Well, A, everything is wet and probably wouldn't burn," Miriam said. "B, we don't have any way to even *start* a fire. And C, even if the first two weren't true, the rising water would probably put it out before morning anyway."

"It was a good thought though, baby," Lara said to him, gently patting his arm like he was a loyal little yappy dog that needed reassurance he was a good boy. Although Lucas did look dejected that his idea wouldn't work, he also looked proud that his girlfriend had acknowledged his idea. Not for the first time, Simon suspected he wasn't the brightest person among the survivors.

Simon stared at the pile of debris and started putting it all together in his mind. This was definitely nowhere near the ideal number or kinds of materials to do anything helpful, but he didn't think this stuff was completely useless, either. Before he could think on it further, though, Katherine drew his attention back to the sharks circling them in the water.

"They can't really be, like, actually dangerous, right?" Katherine asked. "I thought I heard somewhere that most shark species wouldn't actually be a threat to humans, or something like that."

"Well, it's not like they're great whites," Simon said. "They're not capable of chomping you in half in one bite. And you're right, there are quite a few shark species that would just as soon leave humans alone. But these bull sharks are big enough that they could perceive us as prey if they were hungry enough."

"What are the odds that they've just had a big meal and would therefore ignore us?" Miriam asked.

"Sharks aren't specifically my thing, but if I had to guess?" Simon said. "I would say that seeing them this far up the Amazon River is a bad sign. They're going to go where the food is, and if the food isn't where it's supposed to be, they'll keep moving until they find it. For them to be this far from their normal territory, I would think maybe their normal food supply was pretty light. They're likely pretty ravenous."

"So if we try to swim out among them, they will attack?" Miriam asked.

"Yeah, and probably with more savageness than we'd normally see from bull sharks," Simon said.

"But you don't know any of that for sure, do you?" Cory asked. "You're just talking out of your ass and guessing."

Simon tried not to let his annoyance with Cory show, especially since Cory was right. "No, I don't know for sure. I'm not a biologist. I'm just someone who's read more than the average number of books about the Amazon."

"One of us could try swimming out, then," Lucas said. "After we rest, to make sure we have the strength for it."

Simon almost said this was a bad idea, but even if it was a bad idea, it was the only idea they had at the moment. And as their land slowly disappeared into the darkness of the water, they would have to go into the water eventually, one way or the other.

Miriam was the only one who spoke. "Maybe. We should take a short time to think on it, though, see if we can come up with any way to take as much potential danger out of the situation as possible."

"So what are we supposed to do in the meantime?" Cory

asked. "Just sit here? That's an incredibly stupid thing to do. The danger's not going to go away with us just ignoring it."

Ironically enough, ignoring was exactly what pretty much everyone did to Cory's statement.

"Maybe we can try to sleep a little," Lara suggested. "Not for long. I mean, we wouldn't have a lot of time for more than a few power naps."

"It's pouring rain," Lucas complained. "I don't think I could sleep in this."

Somewhere, underneath the dull and constant roar of the rain pouring down on the river, Simon thought he heard something. He almost dismissed it. After all, out there beyond the flooding waters of the river was the actual Amazon River Basin, an enormous rainforest with the highest concentration of life on Earth. It would have been very easy to dismiss any sounds he heard as some kind of wildlife, maybe a jaguar roaring in the night or some kind of night bird.

Then he heard it again.

"Did anyone else catch that?" Simon asked.

"No," Miriam said. "Catch what?"

"I don't know, but it almost sounded like someone else calling out."

"Don't be stupid," Cory said. "There couldn't be…" But he paused and listened. This time, it was apparent from the looks on everyone's faces that they all heard it this time. It was clearly the sound of a human voice calling for help, although Simon couldn't make out what they might be saying.

"Hello?" Miriam cupped her hands around her mouth and called out into the night. She did this several times before they all heard a clear response. Now that he was actually paying close attention to it, the voice sounded like it was trying to say something in Portuguese.

"It's got to be one of the deckhands," Katherine said excitedly. She started to jump up and down, but she slipped in the mud and only kept herself from falling by grabbing onto Miriam's sleeve. "He must have made it to the shore! He can go get help for us!"

But even though Simon couldn't understand what the man was saying, he could clearly hear the panicked tone in his voice. "No. Something's wrong. Wherever he is, he isn't safe."

"Everybody, listen carefully," Miriam said. "See if you can figure out which direction his voice is coming from."

They all listened, and after nearly a minute of bickering and second-guessing, they had more or less a consensus on which direction he was in. Staring long and hard in that direction, Simon started to think he could see a black silhouette of the man against the deeper ebony of the night. "There!" he said, pointing. "Over there. Anyone else see him?"

"He's standing! He *is* on the shore!" Lara said. "And I don't think it's that far away."

For a moment, Simon allowed himself to hope, but the man, now noticing them as well, stood at the edge of the water, waving his arms at them. He certainly didn't sound like he felt he was safe. Disappointment overtook Simon as he realized what had happened.

"He's not on the shore. That's the direction of the other island we thought we saw," Simon said. "And I think maybe it's more into the middle of the river than even ours is. You know, instead of being closer to the shore. He's probably trapped just like us."

"Yeah, and I think maybe he's thinking the same thing we were," Miriam said. "He thinks we're on shore and that we can save him."

Several of the survivors tried to vocally deny it, but as the moments passed, they all realized that was exactly the case. Judging from the way the vague silhouette of the deckhand was pacing, his island might just be a little bit larger, and therefore might stay above the flood for a short time longer than theirs, but in the end, he was just as screwed as them.

They stopped waving at him and trying to get his attention, which he at first seemed to interpret as them giving up on him. He screamed louder in words that, while foreign to Simon's ears, had the universal sound of begging. Soon though, the deckhand's pleas got softer, then eventually stopped altogether. Simon wished he could say something that would get the man to understand that they weren't abandoning him, that they were in just as much danger as him, but instead, he could only hope that the man would figure it out for himself. Eventually, the man's silhouette plopped down into the mud.

It was difficult to hear, but Simon thought he could catch the sounds of the man sobbing. Simon certainly couldn't blame him.

# CHAPTER SEVEN

They all lapsed into silence for some unknown amount of time. The gravity of what had happened to them, and what was still likely to happen, caught up with them, and no matter how determined they were to get out of this, Simon found that his mind forced a moment of mental break. Everyone else, even Cory, seemed to be the same.

After some time had passed, Simon finally realized that the deckhand had stopped his crying and pleading. Standing up from where he had been sitting (and Simon didn't even remember sitting down at any point), he went back to the edge of the island. There was no doubt that the water was farther up the shore now, although it wasn't happening so fast that Simon would notice it if their lives weren't dependent on it. He stood there looking out to the other island, but at first, he couldn't see the other man. After spending some time squinting, he realized the deckhand was now lying down near the center of his island, possibly sleeping on his side. Simon considered calling out to him and getting the man to confirm that he was indeed still alive, but if he was somehow able to get some kind of real rest through all this, Simon didn't want to bother him.

The other possibility was that the man was dead, and if that was the case, Simon would rather not confirm that for sure yet. He didn't know the deckhand in any way, shape, or form, but Simon would prefer if there were no more deaths tonight.

Somehow, he missed the sound of someone coming up behind him until that person put a hand on his shoulder, and Simon jumped, as well as made a distinctly unmanly screech, in surprise. He turned to see Lucas towering behind him. Even though the young man's size should have made him intimidating, the general effect was ruined by the lost-puppy look on Lucas's face. Even before Lucas said anything, Simon realized Lucas had already made the decision that Simon, since he seemed to know more about their situation than anyone else, had to be the one in charge. Again, it was not a position Simon wanted at all, but by now, he was pretty sure that any chance he'd had to pass the buck onto someone else was gone.

"So?" Lucas asked him. There was so much loaded expectation in that single word, and it made Simon uncomfortable. Miriam wandered over to stand next to him, though, and that somehow made Simon feel just a tad stronger.

"So what?" Simon replied back.

"So what's the plan?" Lucas asked. "We've got a plan, right?"

Simon again looked over at the conglomeration of debris they'd collected in the middle of the island. It was, Simon thought, enough to make a very loose, very rickety raft, but not one that would be strong enough to carry any single one of them to safety, let alone all of them. It especially wouldn't be enough to help them considering how fast the river was flowing with the downpour. Simon did think that, if there was anything at all they could do, it would be with that haphazard pile, but he still wasn't entirely sure what. And he could tell from the look on Lucas's face that he wasn't ready for that kind of answer. He wanted some kind of reassurance, and he wanted it immediately.

Even though he knew it would be the wrong answer, Simon said, "The best option at the moment is to wait. If we're lucky, the rain will slow or stop at least long enough for us to see daylight, and then from there, we'll have a better idea of how far it is to shore."

As though he himself were a shark that had sensed blood in the water, Cory was immediately standing and joining their confab. Katherine was close behind him. "Wait?" Cory asked. "That's seriously your answer?"

"Do you have a better one?" Miriam asked him.

"Hey, guys?"

The two words came from the opposite end of the small island, where Lara was standing at the edge of the water and looking out across the darkness. "What is it, baby?" Lucas called to her.

"I think the sharks are gone," Lara said. "I don't see any of their fins. Maybe now's our chance to try swimming."

Simon hissed in a breath as Lara stooped low at the water's edge. "I don't think we should be making that assumption yet." He wanted to tell her she should get away from the river, but she was right. All the fins had disappeared for the moment. Maybe this really would be their chance to escape. He started toward her, and the rest, whether consciously or not, followed.

Lara reached out into the cold waters lapping at the disappearing shore. It was the last voluntary movement she ever made.

A burst of violence exploded from the edge of the water, soaking everybody and blinding most of them to what happened next. Simon hadn't thought it would be possible for the bull shark to get close enough to their shore to do such a thing, especially without its dorsal fin showing, but apparently, the water beyond the edge was deeper than he thought. The huge predator launched itself out of the water with its maw wide open, the ring of razor-blade teeth surrounding Lara's forearm before she could even consider pulling it back. The shark's mouth closed, and with its momentum, it had ripped off her arm and pulled it into the water before she could even fully open her mouth to scream. In the rain-blackened night, the massive jets of blood spurting from her severed arm didn't even look red, but instead like some obsidian substance that had no business coming out of a human being. She toppled into the mud at the edge of the water, and it wasn't until she made a slight splash that any noise left her lips. It still wasn't a scream, though. It was more like an "Oh!" of shock, the sound of someone caught off guard whose body still hadn't realized it was supposed to be in intense pain. The only scream Simon heard was from Lucas as he ran across their island in an effort to reach his girlfriend. He slipped in the mud and fell flat on his ass, preventing him from getting anywhere near her in time.

Miriam and Simon also made a move toward her, but Simon pulled Miriam back from the water as another shark, now no longer hiding its fin, got unnaturally close to the shore, leaped out of the water, and snapped in Lara's direction. Although its teeth missed her, the bull shark's bulk hit her and knocked her deeper into the water, where the spurting blood from her severed arm created a pool to further attract the sharks. Simon froze, unable to do much else but watch. Even Lucas, still screaming his girlfriend's name, seemed reluctant to get anywhere near the water.

Even if he would have tried, he would have swiftly found it impossible to reach Lara without putting himself in extreme danger. The second shark had circled around to make another run at Lara, who in her blind, blood-spurting panic, was flailing her way deeper into the water rather than moving closer to the shore.

More fins popped up, showing the horrified survivors a grand total of five sharks swarming around them, and they all immediately went for Lara. One must have sunk its teeth into something of hers below the water, because she was suddenly yanked far enough out that she could no longer stand. The darkened night and black water were probably a mercy to the horrified observers, as Simon couldn't imagine how much blood currently surrounded the screaming, crying girl. Something yanked her below the surface for a second before she came back up again, sputtering water and desperately trying to breathe. Another yank held her down for longer. This time, when she came back up, there was a huge gouge in the side of her neck and the lower portion of her face. The meat and muscle below her cheekbone were clearly visible, and her eye appeared to be loose in its socket, like the bite had broken the part of her cheekbone and skull that held it in.

"Pleeeeeeease!" she screamed. "Help! I don't want... I don't want to…"

A dorsal fin came speeding at her from behind, and the sound she made as the shark hit her was something that Simon was positive would haunt his dreams for as long as he might live. There was a splash and an audible thump, then her screams for help turned into a wet gurgle. Blood fountained from her mouth. Her body raised up enough in the water for the onlookers to get the shortest glimpse of the damage the shark had done to her torso. The bite had crushed her ribcage and ripped out a large chunk of her back. A pulsing, ravaged organ could be seen within the wound, and despite Simon trying to force his mind not to identify it, he knew that was her lung.

The view was brief, though, as that was the point Lara got yanked down under the water one last time. This time, she didn't come back up.

For several seconds, the only sound was the water of the river as it calmed down from the violence and the pitter-patter of the rain upon their heads. The five dorsal fins all dove completely under the water, and Simon thought he saw the very edge of one tip zooming away from the island. The silence was only broken when Lucas said, improbably, "Lara? Lara, are you alright?"

It might have been a stupid thing to ask, and yet Simon almost understood. What they had just witnessed had been so quick, so terrible and violent, that he didn't blame Lucas for instantly going into a complete state of denial. Simon opened his mouth to reply, then closed it, not knowing if there was anything he could or should say in this situation.

"Lara, please, honey," Lucas said. "Answer me. You're scaring me."

Amazingly, Lara did answer, just not in the way anyone would have wanted her to.

Not too far from where she had gone under, a short distance away as the flow of the river went, something bobbed to the surface. Simon's mind refused to properly acknowledge it at first and insisted it had to be a buoy or a beach ball or something, even if there was no way such objects could have gotten there. Only when Katherine screamed at the sight was Simon forced to recognize it for what it really was.

Other than the chunk of her face that was missing, there was remarkably little damage to Lara's head. Her hair billowed out around her, and there was a permanently shocked expression formed into her face. Below the neck, however, everything was gone, torn away and devoured by the bull sharks.

The head bobbed in the water for several seconds, as though Lara was saying her final goodbye. Then the current of the Amazon River took it, sweeping it away into the darkness of the night and vanishing forever.

Several more seconds passed. Then Lucas spoke again. "Lara, honey, are you okay?"

# CHAPTER EIGHT

The only good thing about the waters coming up higher and higher on the land, as far as Simon could tell, was that it was erasing the last signs of Lara's horrifying struggle. The rain had already done much to wash away her blood, but there had still been smears in the mud showing where she had tried to dig in against the pull of the shark. And no one, whether it was because they hadn't noticed it or simply wanted to ignore it, made mention of the shock of her hair they'd seen floating at the water's edge that was still attached to part of her scalp. It got caught in the mud and stayed there for far too long before the rain and river washed it away.

*Here one moment and gone the next*, Simon thought. Even though it was such a basic concept, it was difficult for him to wrap his mind around it. He hadn't known the girl at all, so to his trauma-ravaged brain, her death was an almost academic concept rather than a full-on tragedy, but he also knew that reaction wouldn't last long. Her death would be something he would see in his dreams every night for the rest of his life.

Assuming, of course, that the rest of his life was longer than just tonight.

When Simon finally came back enough to his senses, he

looked around at the others to see how they were handling the recent horrific events. Lucas, understandably, was the worst off out of all the survivors. That was usually what happened when someone watched their lover get ripped apart by swimming razor blades. He was still staring numbly at the spot where Lara had last gone under the surface as though he expected her to still come back up, even all these minutes later. Miriam and Katherine were sitting down in the mud and huddled together, each of them trying to use the other to keep warm. Cory was the only one other than Simon who seemed like he was up for trying to talk this through, as he paced back and forth on the highest, most-centered point of their so-called island. Reluctantly, Simon went over to Cory and cleared his throat to catch the young man's attention.

"Go away," Cory said.

Simon looked around himself. Where exactly did Cory expect him to go? Going away here would have to consist of walking all of three or four feet. Cory saw him looking and shook his head as though Cory had to be the biggest dumbass in the world. "What I meant was I want to be alone."

"Just hear me out for a second," Simon said. "I wanted to apologize to you."

Cory raised his eyebrow, then gestured for Simon to continue.

"Maybe we shouldn't have pushed you out of the group earlier," Simon said. "You're in the same situation as the rest of us, and you're probably just as traumatized as—"

"I'm not traumatized," Cory said.

Now it was Simon's turn to raise his eyebrows in dismay.

"I'm not," Cory said again. "I don't get traumatized. I'm not weak like that. The rest of you, maybe, but not me. As far as pushing me away, that's exactly what I'm used to from people. Others see that I'm better than them, and they're threatened. I don't blame any of you for that, but that doesn't mean I forgive you."

Simon didn't have much urge to continue speaking to him, but the longer they talked, the more Simon felt they all needed to stick together, Cory included, if they were going to find a way to survive this.

"What's your deal, anyway?" Simon asked.

"What, you think I have an attitude problem or some shit?" Cory asked.

"Well, that, but also, I can't really even figure out how you ended up here. The rest of us all had our reasons for coming to the Amazon, but you don't seem to have one. You're just here. There has to be a story to that."

For a moment, Cory looked stricken in a way that Simon had not seen from him yet. He quickly covered it back up, but in that brief time, Simon had a glimpse of the actual human being underneath the angry, egotistical exterior.

"What does it matter to you?" Cory asked. "Under your leadership, we're all about to die soon anyway, so who cares how we got into this mess?"

"I keep telling you, I'm not the..." Simon sighed. "You know what? Never mind. Forget I even tried to care about you."

He turned and started to walk away (although, again, it wasn't like he could go more than a few feet without either running into the others or walking right into the river), but before he could finish his (mostly symbolic) gesture, Cory put a hand on his shoulder and stopped him.

"Wait. Do you really want to know?"

Simon paused to honestly ask himself that question, then nodded. "Yeah. I really do."

"My father and soon-to-be stepmother forced me to come here. They said I could have a trip anywhere in the world that I wanted, but only on one condition."

"Which was?"

"It had to be this week, so that I wouldn't be anywhere near their wedding."

"Wait, really?"

"Are you accusing me of lying? Of course, really. My stepmother hates me. I never forgave my father for cheating on my mother, and I'm vocal about it. So they sent me off on the first trip they could find on short notice, and I ended up here, stuck on a rock in the middle of the water with you assholes. So there. You know my tragic origin story. Now would you kindly go stick your nose in someone else's shit?"

Simon took a step back. Okay, yeah, he supposed that would be enough to give anyone a chip on his shoulder about what others might consider a dream vacation. He wanted to know more, especially since he was a little confused about why a man presumably in his twenties had to be sent away by his father and stepmother like he was a misbehaving child. Couldn't Cory have just not taken the vacation and avoided the wedding? Still, it was enough of a sob story that Simon didn't want to push any further and potentially cause more harm. Instead, Simon gave Cory his peace, or at least as much as was possible in the current situation, and instead went to check on the others. Miriam seemed to be mostly back to her senses, even though she kept staring at the place in the water where Lara had disappeared. Katherine was still sitting and sobbing quietly into her hands.

Lucas, understandably, was the one who seemed the most affected. He stood at the edge of the water, inching back every so often so that the water wouldn't touch him as though he would be in danger if the river so much as touched his toe. Every so often, he would call out Lara's name to the river, but the tone kept changing so that Simon wasn't sure if he was still calling for her to come back or if he were just lamenting what had happened. Simon approached him cautiously, afraid to disturb him in much the same way he would be afraid to disturb a sleepwalker. He could picture Lucas startling and hitting him or throwing him in the river. And even though the sharks were not currently visible, Simon thoroughly believed they were still there.

"Lucas?" Simon asked him softly.

At first, Lucas acted like he hadn't heard. Then, equally as quiet as though he were trying not to wake someone up, Lucas said, "How long do you think it's going to be before she comes back?"

*Oh dear Lord*, Simon thought. He had never actually seen someone in this much shock. He hadn't even thought it was actually a real-life thing. "Lucas, she's not," Simon said. "She's gone. She's dead."

After several seconds, Lucas nodded slowly, but he didn't turn away from watching the river. "She's been starting to drop hints that maybe I should give her a ring at some point, you know?"

Simon didn't know what else he was supposed to do in response except listen quietly.

"I love her, but I don't know if I love her *that* much. And she isn't finished with college yet. Me, I don't really care if I finish, but she's smarter than me. She could actually be something. And maybe, if we were married, I'd get in the way of that."

Simon waited for several seconds to see if he was finished before he spoke. "Lucas, maybe you should come away from the water. Whatever we're going to do, we should probably try doing it rested. If all of us huddle together, we might all be able to fit under Katherine's poncho and get some sleep without the rain waking us."

Lucas shook his head. "Can't sleep. Lara might come back. I

should be waiting for her if she does."

The image again popped in Simon's brain of Lara's head bobbing to the surface of the river and then floating away. He'd been trying to avoid thinking about it, but now that he did, he realized he had been able to see the muscle and bones in her neck, as well as a hole that had probably been her esophagus.

"She's not coming back, Lucas. She's dead."

Lucas's lip quivered, but he didn't cry. "Maybe."

"No maybe, Lucas."

"Just… just let me wait here for just a little longer. Just in case, you know?"

Simon wasn't sure if it was healthy to indulge him, but he also knew it wouldn't be helpful at all trying to force Lucas to deal with this any quicker. At least he was maybe coming out of it a little bit.

He turned back to the others. In truth, what he had just told Lucas about what he intended to do hadn't even been in his mind before it left his mouth, but now that it had, Simon saw some logic to it.

"We should try to get some sleep," Simon said.

"That's your plan on what to do next?" Cory asked. "Go to bed and hope that the problem goes away?"

"No," Simon said. "The problem's not going to go away. But if we don't get some rest, our ability to actually do something about the problem is going to be hampered. We all need to be able to look at the problem with something that's at least related to fresh eyes."

"It's pouring rain," Miriam said. "I kind of doubt that I'll be able to sleep in this."

"We'll all stay together for warmth and stay under the poncho to keep the rain out of our faces. We only do this for maybe an hour or two. Even if we don't actually fall asleep, the rest will do us good."

"Stupid idea," Cory muttered. "If you three want to lie down in the mud and pretend there isn't a problem, then be my guest. But I'm not having anything to do with this."

Simon looked to Miriam and Katherine to see whether they would go along with it. Katherine, in turn, looked to Miriam, who was giving Simon a long, appraising glare.

"Okay," Miriam finally said. "The other two can stay awake and keep an eye on the water level, maybe wake us up if it rises quicker than we thought it would." She looked at Cory for confirmation, who sullenly shrugged before nodding. She and Katherine tried to make something like a soft place to rest in the mud, then let Simon join them. "But I'm telling you, I really don't think I'm going to be able to sleep after everything that's happened."

But she was wrong. All three of them fell into a restless sleep within minutes of pulling the poncho over their heads.

# CHAPTER NINE

They were asleep. The idiots were actually asleep. Sure, Cory supposed he could see the wisdom in getting some rest, considering he himself was feeling quite punchy by this point. But with Simon, Miriam, and Katherine all under the poncho and at least one of them snoring away, that left Cory to take back control of his own fate from this gang of incredible dumbasses.

Before he did anything, he crept closer to the three prone forms under the poncho and listened very closely to their breathing, making absolutely sure they were asleep. One of them, that Katherine chick, was snoring lightly, while the other two slept quietly. The way they were positioned, the poncho didn't immediately block their ability to breathe, but it could be adjusted very easily to suffocate all of them at once. Cory took special note of that, but he didn't actually act on it. Not yet, at least. He still wasn't sure if killing each and every one of them was the best thing under this situation. He would have to give it some more thought. Besides, if he really did decide that every single other survivor of the boat needed to die, then the first would have to be that lumbering oaf Lucas. He was the biggest physical threat, so he would have to be taken care of first.

While Cory knew he hadn't done much to hide his nature

from this particular group, he was pretty certain that none of them was completely aware of how much of a danger he truly was. That Simon shithead had even seemed to buy his bullshit sob story about his father and stepmother. Most of it was a lie, of course. He didn't have a woman about to be his stepmother. That would have required his father to still be alive. The one part of the story that had been true was that his father had cheated on his mother. He'd just neglected to mention the part where his mother had murdered the man for it while Cory had been forced to watch back when he'd been in second grade. Far from being horrified by it, Cory had been fascinated, and that fascination had continued on into his adult life.

And that fascination was also the reason he was here. After all, he'd needed to run somewhere after he'd committed his first murder, and faking being a tourist in a faraway country had seemed like as good a cover story as any while he waited for the heat from his crime to cool down. Thinking back on it now, though, he would have put a little more thought into which trip he took rather than simply taking the first, cheapest one he could find. It was a mistake he would have to be sure not to make again, assuming he made it off this floating mudball alive.

And surviving this situation was exactly what he intended to do. He just didn't think he'd be able to do it with so many of the other survivors contradicting his obvious superiority in decision making. It was definitely time to thin the group out, he figured, if he wanted to give himself a better chance at making his way out of this.

Leaving the three sleeping beauties, Cory stood up and went over to Lucas. The grieving boyfriend had come out of his strange fugue of denial long enough to come closer into the center of the island, but he was still clearly out of sorts. Keeping his voice low, so quiet that Lucas almost wouldn't be able to hear him over the rain, he said, "Lucas? I need to speak to you. It's important." He wasn't even sure if the dumbass actually heard him, but when Cory put a hand on his arm to lead him, the oaf followed like a puppy on a leash.

With Lucas at his side, Cory led them as far away from their tiny excuse for a camp as possible. Given the ever-shrinking nature of their tiny refuge, it wasn't much in the way of solitude, but if he did it carefully enough, Cory figured he could still do what he needed to do and none of the others would be the wiser.

Lucas stopped at the edge, and although it was difficult to be certain in the darkness and rain, Cory thought the guy may have actually stopped right around the point where Lara had last been seen before finding out her place in the food chain. Cory had been shocked by the sudden violence of her death just as much as any of the others, but he also suspected that he was the one who had recovered from it the quickest. She'd been a bitch, after all. All of them were, every single person who'd been on that boat that wasn't him. It was something Cory had grown used to by this point in his life. Every single person was an asshole, a useless shitstain upon the world. And yes, he understood that "everyone" included himself. He had come to grips with that long ago, just as he had long ago realized he had to look out for himself over anyone else. And one of the things he had realized he needed to do in order to survive was reduce the number of people that would be a drain on their limited resources here on this tiny patch of land.

And Lucas, he decided now, would be the easiest to get rid of first. He was so out of it from seeing his girlfriend die that he wasn't paying any attention to anything else around him. But also, if he got his act back together, he was the largest and most physically imposing of the group, with almost as much height as Cory, as well as more muscle. The last thing Cory wanted was to deal with this asshole later.

Cory looked over at the other three. They were all still huddled together under Katherine's poncho, sleeping fitfully even as the rain plopped down on top of them. The rain might cover most sounds Cory made during this, but he would still need to be careful. Too much noise and they would definitely hear.

Once the two of them were as far away from the others as was possible on their incredible shrinking island, Cory whispered, "Look, I've got to tell you, I'm worried about the others."

Lucas looked more confused and lost than before, if such a thing was even possible. "Why would you be worried?" The way he said it, it was almost as though he had forgotten that all of them were in danger.

Cory knew it was taking a risk, but he thought he could take advantage of Lucas's clearly confused and traumatized state. "I'm afraid one of them might try to go after Lara and get her back."

The ideal situation here would be for Lucas to still be so shell-shocked—or so stupid, as the case might be—that he would still be somewhat convinced that Lara might be alive. Unfortunately for Cory, Lucas's grief seemed to have evolved past that point.

"Simon said she's dead," Lucas said. "And I think maybe he's right. I'm suddenly remembering stuff I wasn't for a bit. I think… I think maybe I saw her head…"

Oh no, this wouldn't do. Cory tried to steer him back away from any kind of clear-headed reasoning. "Don't listen to Simon. You only think you saw that because of how dark it is. I'm telling you, I heard her calling out for help only a couple minutes ago. I think she might be on an island just a little further down the river."

Cory's attempts to convince him seemed to be having the

opposite effect. "Cory, I don't know what you think you're doing. Maybe you're trying to make me feel better, but…"

"But nothing. I'm not the only one who heard it," Cory said. "The others did, too. Simon was whispering to me about it. The three of them are going to try a rescue attempt when they wake up."

Cory didn't know whether Lucas was actively stupid or just desperate for some kind of hope, but he could see a glimmer of something appear in the man's eyes. "You're serious?"

"Yeah, but I don't think any of them would be able to save her. They didn't want to tell you yet because they knew you would go rushing headlong after her, and you definitely need to not do that, but I'm not sure if any of them have the strength to…"

Ah, now Cory could see that he was getting to the oaf. "You don't get to tell me what I need to do and don't need to do. I'm the one who decides, and Lara's my girlfriend, not anyone else's. If someone's going to save her, it should be me."

Oh lordy, this was working far better now than Cory had expected. Maybe he wouldn't even have to physically do anything to take this guy out of the equation. He honestly looked like he was going to swim out into the middle of a raging river that they all knew was full of sharks, just because someone had told him his clearly dead girlfriend might still be alive on some unknown island out there in the dark. Lucas would do this, and then Cory could get rid of Simon. With the two other men gone, he'd be left with the two easily pliable women who would do what he said, allowing them to finally get out of here. Hell, after they were off the island, he might even let the women live long enough to get back to civilization, if that suited him.

Although he doubted it. In truth, the isolation would be the perfect cover to kill them too and do whatever he wanted with them. All he'd have to do when he reached safety was say they'd died in the river along with everyone else. Hell, this trip might even end up being fun after all.

Cory looked around at the dark water, searching for any signs of the sharks. They had already shown that their dorsal fins wouldn't necessarily be above the water just before a kill, so Cory couldn't be sure, but it didn't look like any of them were in the immediate vicinity. The three sleepers still seemed to be out, and there was even still silence from the other island somewhere out there in the dark, if its sole habitant was even still alive.

Lucas started to walk into the water, and Cory noticed the way the water here tried to swiftly pull away anything that entered it. Even if the sharks didn't finish the job for him, the river was likely to sweep Lucas away and take him out of the picture the instant he tried to swim in it. But as Lucas waded out to just below his shin, he stopped and turned to Cory.

"I shouldn't be doing this," Lucas said. "It's not going to work."

"But Lara could be—" Cory began, but he didn't get far before Lucas cut him off.

"Lara's dead. I saw her die. I… I think I've been in denial. Or shock. Or…"

Before he could say anything else, Cory shoved him. Lucas, completely unprepared for this, stumbled backward in the water and fell flat on his back in the shallows. Cory didn't give him any chance to try getting back up. Immediately, the skinnier man was on top of Lucas's chest with his hands around Lucas's neck and holding the larger man's head just under the water. Lucas struggled, but Cory's position kept him from getting any leverage over the attacker.

As Lucas's attempts to get Cory off him grew more feeble, Cory looked around again, sure that he was going to need to contend with one of the others now. Lucas's splash, however, hadn't seemed to be any louder to the sleepers than the rain on the poncho over their head, since all three of them stayed exactly as they had been.

Lucas stopped moving, but Cory didn't get off him yet. He could see fins now further out in the water, and he knew he needed to get back to relatively dry land before they made a bee-line over here, but he wasn't going to take any chances with this oaf. He waited until he was absolutely certain that Lucas was dead, then stood up and shoved Lucas deeper into the water with his foot. The current took his body, and true to form, the sharks went after it. They were too far from the island for anyone to hear signs of their feeding frenzy this time, though.

After taking a moment to shake himself off and let the adrenaline of the kill have its euphoric way with his body, Cory once more went over to the others and considered them. If he really wanted them dead, this would be the perfect time to do it. It would certainly be the smartest way. And yet, despite the desperate situation he found himself in, Cory couldn't help but think this was fun. Not one of them suspected how dangerous he truly was, and while killing Simon and possibly the girls now would have been the easiest course of action, he couldn't help but want to extend this little game for a longer period of time.

Rest assured, he was the only one of them who would walk out of the Amazon River Basin alive. But, in the meantime, he could be the cat toying with his catch. He could take them out later, one by one, when it was fun. None of them would be ready.

For now, though, the act of killing had made him tired. Using part of his shirt to protect his head from the rain, Cory joined the other three in the mud and allowed a temporary sleep to overtake him. When next he woke, the fun would continue.

# CHAPTER TEN

With how distracted everyone was with their own misery, it wasn't a surprise that Simon didn't realize Lucas was missing until he had been awake for nearly ten minutes. That didn't make him feel any less bad about it later, though. With only about thirty square feet of land for them to be on at that point, missing an entire person for ten minutes was a pretty big deal.

He shook Katherine awake, but hesitated before doing the same with Cory. The guy was in the same boat, so to speak, as the rest of them, so he had a right to know that something was wrong, but Simon almost wanted to leave him out of the loop. If Lucas was truly gone, then Simon suspected that the first words out of Cory's mouth would be something unthinking, uncaring, and insensitive, and Simon simply couldn't bring himself to listen to any of that right now.

"What is it?" Katherine murmured sleepily to him. By her side, Miriam also stirred.

"Lucas is gone," Simon said quietly to her. Miriam, despite being the groggier of the two women, immediately sat up in a flash and blinked at him.

"What do you mean he's gone?" Miriam asked.

"I mean he's gone. What else is there I could mean?"

She stood up and looked around at their island, but it had

shrunk even more as they slept and there weren't exactly any places for someone to hide. "Lucas?" she called out into the night. Simon joined her, although it felt kind of silly, screaming out someone's name in order to look for them on a patch of land that, at the moment, was probably roughly five hundred square feet. If they couldn't immediately see him, then it simply wasn't possible that he was here. They might as well be in as much denial as when Lucas himself had been calling out for someone who was clearly no longer among the living.

"This doesn't make any sense," Katherine said. There was a distinctly haunted note in her voice, and Simon couldn't blame her for it. Everything that had already happened to them so far tonight was horrible, but up until now, they'd had some kind of explanation for each new piece of their misery. The inexplicable and unknown, however, was so much more terrifying. Whether it was logical or not, Simon couldn't help but imagine himself suddenly vanishing into the void with no rhyme or reason behind it. "Did he manage to swim away? Wouldn't we have heard that?"

Simon looked back out at the last place he had seen the shark fins prowling the waters. They weren't there now, but they had already seen that just because the fins weren't visible didn't mean the sharks weren't present. "Maybe," Simon said noncommittally. "Maybe not. But I think we need to assume that whatever happened, we're not going to see him again. Either he escaped and avoided doing anything to let us know, or he drowned, or he was eaten."

Cory snorted. They all turned to look at the young man, who was once again awake and watching them. "Idiot probably thought he saw his girlfriend and dove after her, if you ask me."

Everyone else turned away from him, the unspoken implication being that no one had asked him, nor did they care about his opinion.

"So, what? That's it?" Katherine asked. "We're just going to write off Lucas and be all, 'Oops, he's gone, whatever?' We're not going to do anything at all to try to find out what happened?"

"What are we even supposed to do?" Miriam asked her. "Call the cops? Have them break out a forensics kit?"

"No, it's just... all we're doing is sitting here! Lucas disappeared, and we all slept through it, for Christ's sakes!"

"Bickering is not going to solve anything," Simon said, but he had difficulty putting any conviction in his voice. To him, this somehow felt worse than having to watch as one of their own had been ripped apart by sharks. In that case, it had been something they'd known and understood. He could quantify it when someone's body was eaten and had her head sent floating down the Amazon. But even though he was certain that Lucas had to be dead now, there was no physical evidence. His disappearance would likely remain a mystery, just one more thing about this whole trip that would haunt him for the rest of his life, if that life even proved to be longer than another day.

Even though he hadn't sounded that convincing to his own ears, both Katherine and Miriam stopped arguing, and instead went to hugging each other close where they sat. It truly looked like there was nothing any of them could do, but Simon still had something like a plan. It probably wasn't a very good one, but it was better to be doing something in an attempt to better their situation than it was to sit around worrying. And now that he had a little sleep, even as unrestful as it had been, he thought he might be able to think more clearly as he tried to work. He started to put all the pieces of debris and driftwood he had gathered together in a row, then went back around the edge of their island looking for more. There wasn't much, but he did find a particularly long branch, almost eight feet in length, that he suspected could be put to a particular use. He set that aside, then started weaving their small, pathetic piece of rope through the wood. Simon was definitely not an outdoorsy type, so he doubted how strong his craftsmanship on this would be, but he knew a few knots and had some basic engineering knowledge, enough that he thought he could turn this all into a raft that would support the weight of at least one person.

"What is that even supposed to be?" Katherine asked him.

"I'm trying to make a raft."

"You're not going to be able to make a raft out of that garbage," Cory said.

"Cory, just shut your hole, alright?" Miriam said. "If you're not going to contribute, then just stay out of the way." She paused for just a second before saying to Simon, "He's right, though."

Simon shot her a glare that told her exactly what he thought of her helpful statement.

"What I mean is, what you have here won't be able to make much," Miriam said. "When I was a kid, I used to make a bunch of toy boats and float them down the river in my hometown. I would put my teddy bears on them. But heavier things like Barbie's dream house wouldn't stay on because of buoyancy or something. I lost a lot of Barbies that way."

"Somewhere in there, I almost thought I heard useful advice," Simon said.

"I guess I'm saying that I might be able to help," Miriam said. She got down in the mud and inspected what he had set down, rearranging a couple pieces of driftwood and boat debris. "See, if you put this part out on the sides, maybe it will…"

"Hey, you guys ever hear of that plane with a soccer team that crashed in the mountains?" Katherine asked. She was staring out at the water as she said it, watching as one of the shark fins popped up, leisurely circled the island for a short time, and then vanished again.

"Uh, no," Miriam said. Simon thought it sounded vaguely familiar, like maybe he had seen a movie about it a long time ago.

"It was, like, in the Andes or something," Katherine said. "This team crashed and they were stuck, and you know, it's freezing up there so there's not a lot of plants or animals to hunt or anything. And a lot of the team died in the crash, so they had these frozen bodies sitting around. So the soccer players had no choice but to go cannibal and eat the dead people."

"Ew," Miriam commented. She wasn't paying that much attention, though, instead continuing to work side by side with Simon.

"And what exactly is your point?" Cory asked.

"My point is, uh, I'm pretty hungry."

Everyone stopped what they were doing and stared at her.

"Wait, no! I'm not trying to imply that any of us should try killing and eating each other," Katherine said. "But that is something we haven't worried about yet. We have nothing to eat. There's water to drink, I guess, but shouldn't we be planning something too to keep ourselves fed?"

"This island is going to disappear beneath the surface of the river long before we have to worry about starving to death," Miriam said. "And if we manage to get to land, there's animals and plants."

"Animals that want to eat us and plants that are probably poisonous," Cory pointed out.

"My point being that we're not going to starve," Miriam said. "At least not right away. So we don't have to worry about the horrible fate of becoming a soccer team."

Katherine quieted after that, and all there was to do was work on the raft. And all the while, the shark fins started to pop up more and more frequently, as though something had sated their appetites for a while but they were now ready for their next snack.

Simon tried not to consider that it might be him.

# CHAPTER ELEVEN

Although Simon wasn't sure exactly how long it took them to fiddle with the raft, he knew it took longer than he had hoped. Even with two people working on it together, it was still difficult to assemble the contraption in the dark with the rain still falling mercilessly and making it difficult for them to hold onto anything without it slipping from their fingers. Eventually, they finished, and Simon and Miriam stood up and stepped away so the entire group could survey what they had created.

Katherine dubiously poked the conglomeration of sticks and driftwood with her toe. "There's no way in hell this thing is going to support all four of us, much less protect any of us from the bull sharks."

"Well, we don't need it to support all four," Simon said. "We just need it to support one."

"And what good is a raft for only one of us going to do?" Cory asked. "Are you planning to take it to shore and then, what, push it back in the hope it gets back to this damned patch of land?"

"Shore's not the only destination we have as an option," Simon said. "In fact, it's not even the closest." He pointed back along the waters where they had come from, indicating the shadowy bulk partially sticking out of the water that was all that remained of their boat. As the waters had risen, more and more of it sunk below the surface, but a significant portion of it was still just barely visible in the darkness.

"The boat?" Cory asked. "What the hell do you expect to be able to do with the boat? You're not going to patch it up and sail us all out of here."

"Quit being an asshole," Miriam said. "I get what Simon's thinking. There's got to still be supplies over there, things we might be able to use to survive. Am I right?"

"Right," Simon said. "Even if most of it washed away, any tiny thing we find might be useful, and not just here on the island."

"Yeah, I guess none of us have really thought about that yet."

"Thought about what?" Katherine asked.

"We've been so focused on surviving the island and getting to the shore without being eaten that we haven't even begun to talk about what we might do if we make it to shore," Miriam said. "I mean, other than talking about how to not be a soccer team. Right now, we might still be *on* the Amazon, but if we get off, we'll still be *in* the Amazon. As in, we've got how many hundreds or thousands of miles of rainforest we would still need to get through in order to call ourselves safe."

"So even if we survive the river and the bull sharks, we'll still need some way to survive until we can get out of the jungle," Simon said. "And that means we need more supplies. Any supplies at all."

"Okay, that's interesting," Cory said.

"What's interesting?"

"You almost said and did a smart thing there, thinking ahead. But the key word is almost. You're still an idiot."

"If you don't have anything useful to contribute..." Miriam

started to say, but Cory cut her off.

"The wreck of the boat is up the river from us," Cory said. "I've already seen how fast the flow of the water can wash... things downriver. So while the raft might keep you from being directly in the water with the sharks, how exactly are you planning to guide it against the flow of the river?"

Condescending though Cory may be, it was a good question. Thankfully, it was one that Simon had already considered. He went over to the bits of flotsam and driftwood that he hadn't used to build the raft and held up the one particularly long branch. "I can use this to push the raft along. You know, like those gondolas they have in Venice."

"Are you sure that's going to be long enough?" Katherine asked.

"No," Simon said. "I have no idea how deep the river is at any point, but I do see that the boat is being kept in place by something underneath. So it can't be so deep here that the boat isn't touching bottom. This should be long enough to touch the bottom of the river and push me along, unless I go over a particularly deep section."

"Wait," Miriam said. "Why are you just assuming that the person who's going to take this thing over to the boat is you?"

Simon opened his mouth and then closed it a couple of times before answering. "I just thought no one else would want to do it."

"Bullshit," Cory said. "You want to be the one to do it in order to be the one to get the glory."

"What glory, you asshole?" Miriam asked. "It's not like there's hidden cameras watching us or something. We're not on *Impractical Jokers*."

"You're right," Simon said to Miriam, choosing to completely ignore Cory's accusation. "The raft is going to be pretty weak. The person with the best chance of succeeding on it will be the one who's the lightest. So I think that would be you."

Miriam nodded, but suddenly she didn't look so enthusiastic. "I'm not sure how excited I am to get back in that water, though. Not after watching what happened to Lara."

"Well, I'm certainly not going to do it," Katherine said. "I'm probably the second lightest here, but you couldn't pay me to get anywhere near those sharks without physically picking me up and throwing me in."

"And Cory's definitely not light enough," Simon said. "No offense to you or anything, but you're tall and look like you have a couple extra pounds."

"It's muscle," Cory said with a sniff. "But you're right. Out of the four of us, I'm the heaviest, and that so-called raft you made wouldn't hold up under me for more than half a minute at most."

"So that leaves you and me, Miriam," Simon said. A part of him actually hoped she would be the one to volunteer. She did have the best chance, after all, and he didn't want to get any closer to the water than the rest of them. But although she had seemed at first like she wanted to do it, now Miriam appeared to remember how harrowing the attempt would actually be. Finally, she shook her head and turned away in shame.

"You're right," Miriam said. "I can't do it. I'm sorry I questioned you."

Knowing that his own nerve would disappear if he waited too long, Simon pushed the raft to the edge of the water, then sat down on it and situated himself so he would have the best balance without any part of himself actually hanging over the side and acting like a meaty fishing lure for the bull sharks. Katherine handed him the branch he would use to push himself along, then she and Miriam stooped low and positioned themselves to push the raft into the water. "Ready?" Miriam asked.

"No, wait. Just give me a moment," Simon said. All of a sudden he was paralyzed by fear. Did he really want to try doing this? The raft was truly a pathetic little thing, only barely big enough to float beneath him. And here he was trying to use it to go against the flow of the river toward a boat that might not even have anything useful for them, all while surrounded by meat-eating fish that were relatively unchanged from the era of dinosaurs.

Maybe, just maybe, he could instead use the raft and try to abandon the others. He could go the direction he believed to be south instead of heading to the boat, and then he could try to find help for the others from there. It was the smarter thing to do, and the thought lingered in his head for many seconds.

Then the more noble part of himself prevailed and shamed him for even considering that. He couldn't leave the others behind. No matter how much he tried to justify it, he knew that any help he could find on the shore, if such a thing was even anywhere within easy walking distance, would never be found in time to save the others from the rising waters of the Amazon River. He'd come back, if he really came back at all, to find the islands gone and the sharks swimming languidly with full bellies. No, he hadn't wanted to take any kind of leadership position, but now he was in it one way or the other, and he couldn't let anyone else down.

"Okay, now I'm ready," Simon said. "Push me out."

The girls had some trouble getting the raft out of the mud, and once he was floating on the water, he almost lost his balance right away and tumbled into the river, but he regained it quickly and pushed off behind himself with the branch. He didn't have any time to further prepare himself before he already found himself fighting against the flow of the river, and within less than a minute, he already felt an ache in his upper body from trying to guide the raft in a direction even slightly like the one he wanted to take. He wanted to look back and see how much progress he had made, but he was afraid both that he would see he had made very little, and that the action would cause him to lose what little control he had over the raft and send it hurtling down the river in the opposite direction that he wanted to go.

Simon had been able to ignore the rain for most of the night, but now that he was trying to concentrate, every single drop felt like a distraction. The branch was slick and slippery, often threatening to slip right out from his fingers, and his worries about the depths to which the branch could reach quickly proved to be well-founded. He soon had to stab the branch very low into the river in order for it to find any surface underneath on which to find purchase, and if it got much deeper, he would have to start actually reaching under the water. Just as he came to that realization, he also noticed that the majority of visible shark fins were no longer circling the island, but rather were making large, slow turns around him and the raft. Sticking any part of himself in the water would be dangerous. He might very well have to turn back before he had made even the slightest progress.

But even as that thought crossed his mind, he discarded it. He and the other three survivors didn't have a lot of options left. If they wanted to live through the night, they would have to do things that weren't exactly safe. And if that included him being forced to physically stick his hands in the shark-infested waters just to keep the raft moving in somewhat the right direction, then oh well.

He concentrated so much on keeping the raft on course that he didn't even realize how close he was getting to the boat until it started to loom large in his vision. Now that he was closer, it looked worse for wear than it had at a distance. However, he also saw immediately that the trip might actually lead to some good. There were several broken boxes of what might be some kind of supplies that were strewn about on the severe angle of the deck that was still above water, as well as what appeared to be a duffel bag of some sort that was caught in the railing just above the water line. The duffel looked like it could have belonged to one of the tourists, so maybe it would have things they needed. Simon immediately started pushing the raft in that direction, confident that he could...

There was a wordless, high-pitched scream from somewhere behind him. Simon didn't need to look to know that it was coming from their little island.

# CHAPTER TWELVE

Simon gave up trying to get to the boat and turned back. He expected to see that one of the remaining tourists had fallen into the water or something and immediately become prey to one of the sharks. What he hadn't expected to see was Cory grappling with the two girls and trying to drag them to the water as though he intended to throw them in.

If Katherine had been larger, she might have been able to fight off Cory and his much more significant weight. Unfortunately, she was unable to get any leverage as the much larger man grabbed her from behind and locked his arms around her. Simon, unable to do anything but paddle more frantically in his attempt to get back, was forced to watch the melee play out. The way Cory held her, she was completely able to move her arms, making it easy for him to twist and toss her into the water's edge. Miriam screamed, but she didn't move. She seemed caught between wanting to run and help her friend and knowing she had to stay as far away from Cory as possible.

So both Simon and Miriam watched helplessly as the dorsal fins circling the shrinking island immediately turned and made a bee-line for the place where Katherine was wading waist-deep in the river. Katherine, for her part, seemed to realize this was absolutely not the place where she wanted to be, but she was still too dazed by Cory's unexpected attack to make an immediate move back to the limited safety of land. She floundered in the water like she was unsure which direction to swim, either to the relative safety of the land or away from the crazy asshole that had thrown her off of it, and that hesitation cost her. Several circling bull shark fins dove below the surface, followed moments later by a sharp tug on Katherine that temporarily pulled her under the water. She splashed wildly and managed to pull away, but as she got to water shallow enough where she could walk on the bottom, she was noticeably limping. The sharks had managed to do some damage to her, and it was slowing her down. Another dorsal fin popped up thirty feet behind and to her left, then zipped at her with a speed Simon hadn't actually realized was possible in a shark in such shallow water. Katherine screamed as the shark clipped her with its flippers and knocked her over, causing her to mostly go under again.

As this was happening, Cory had made a move to grab Miriam and do the same to her, but Miriam was stronger and more wiry than she looked. She slipped between his arms, dropped low to the ground, and then twisted into exactly the right position to land a sucker punch square in the middle of Cory's crotch. He screeched and almost dropped to his knees, but kept his balance at the last moment and instead staggered away from Miriam. Instead of going in for another blow, she ran to the edge of island and reached out for Katherine, all the while making sure to not so much as let the tip of her toes touch the water.

Simon hadn't even realized how frantically he was now paddling to get back to the island until he felt like he was running out of breath. Even with the flow of the river now working with him rather than against him, though, he got the impression he wasn't going to get there in time to do anything. Even worse, the rickety raft was feeling even more now like it was ready to wimp apart under his weight. He could forget the raft and dive in, probably getting back to the island sooner, but he didn't want to present another target for the sharks.

Not that they weren't too distracted to even pay him any mind. They were swarming near Katherine now, and Simon could see that he was far too late to be able to do anything to save her. Even Miriam, who was significantly closer, wasn't able to get to her in time as a shark rushed through the water and slammed into Katherine's legs from behind. She screamed, but the sound was cut off as she went under the water. The water churned, and Simon didn't have to be nearby to know that the water would be turning red. Katherine was beyond saving, but there was still Miriam.

However, without the element of surprise for Cory, it didn't seem that Miriam necessarily needed Simon's help in order to kick the murderer's ass. Even as she took a brief moment to scream her friend's name, Miriam turned back to Cory and backhanded him across the face. Simon forgot to paddle and try directing his ride as he stopped and admired how the petite young woman expertly rounded on her attacker, going right from one attack to the next, punching him in the stomach, kicking him in the shin, and trying but failing to get another shot off in his crotch. Cory looked almost comical, backing away from this tiny whirling dervish of pure rage. Miriam didn't seem to have any actual training in any sort of martial arts or self-defense, nor did she need it. She was just faster than him.

Finally remembering that he couldn't be of any help if the raft went completely off course and missed the island, Simon used his branch to steer and push himself along, sending him back to where he had started in only a fraction of the time it had taken him to get away. With the sharks still occupied with whatever remained of Katherine, Simon jumped off the raft before it hit shore and pulled it in the rest of the way. His rough handling of it proved to be the final straw, as the rope they'd been using to keep it together finally came untied. Several of the pieces of wood came off and floated away, but that wasn't where Simon's primary concern was at the moment. He almost tripped and fell in the water thanks to his legs underneath him falling asleep while on the raft. Simon managed to keep his balance, though, just long enough to rush at Cory and hit him square in the gut with his shoulder. Miriam had already softened him up pretty well, so Simon's attack was the final blow needed to send Cory flying back into the water.

It almost would have been nice if Simon had hit the bastard off the side of the island where the sharks were currently feeding off their current victim, but instead, Cory splashed down on the exact opposite of the still-shrinking island. He went completely under for just a second before he sat back up, the water shallow enough beneath him that he could sit in the water without drowning. Simon was hesitant to go after him, and for just a moment, it looked like Miriam might not want to attack, either. Then she took an unthinking flying leap at him, landing right on top of him and connecting his face with her fists.

"You bastard! You fucker! You killed her! I'll rip you apart for that! I'll eat your liver! I'll rip off your head and then shit down your—"

"Miriam, no!" Simon screamed. He'd been keeping an eye on the sharks this whole time, and he'd already seen a couple of fins disappear below the water while others started to make their way around the island. "Get back out of the water! They're coming for you!"

For a moment, Miriam didn't seem to hear him. She simply kept pounding away at Cory. Her small fists probably weren't doing much damage, but he obviously hadn't been expecting this much fight from her, for even with his superior size, he seemed to be flailing. "Why?" she screamed in his face. "Why would you do that? You murderous sack of shit! I'm going to rip off your cock and—"

"Miriam!" Simon yelled again. This time, she finally seemed to hear him and realized she was in a dangerous position. She landed one more painful-looking blow to Cory's cheek, then got off him and ran through the shallow part of the water to the shore. Simon tried to grab her and help her, but she shrugged off his hands and turned to watch Cory, obviously expecting to see him suffer the same fate as Katherine within the next few seconds.

Simon, too, thought at first that they were about to witness another bloody feeding frenzy, but from the moment Miriam had left him, Cory was already pushing himself deeper out into the water. From the angle they were currently coming, the sharks had to swim against the flow of the river. Considering they were in their element, they could obviously do that a lot faster than any human could, but it did slow them down just enough. Cory didn't have to fight the flow as much, as he was swimming for the other island that was currently home to the deckhand.

"He's getting away!" Miriam said. "There has to be something we can do to stop him."

Simon could tell from her face, though, that she knew very well that they wouldn't be able to do anything to help or hinder Cory at the moment, not that he would be able to get far. His larger and more athletic body propelled him along just enough to barely stay out of range of the bull sharks. Simon wouldn't have thought it possible, but maybe, considering the sharks had just had another full meal, they weren't so eager to rip into new prey so soon. Whatever the reason, Cory kept swimming into the dark, and soon they saw his soaking form rising up on the shore of the other island.

Even with Cory well out of their way and no longer any danger to them, Miriam stood on the edge of their island, her body tense like she was ready for a fresh fight. She continued to scream across the distance to him. "Why? Are you going to fucking answer me or not?"

Cory didn't. In fact, now that he wasn't even on the same island as them, he didn't even acknowledge their presence. He nonchalantly wandered over to the prone form of the deckhand and inspected him. Whatever he saw must not have interested him that much, as he soon wandered away again and found a place to sit in the middle of the island. He even looked like he was about to go to sleep.

"Answer me already, you bastard!" Miriam screamed. For a moment, Simon was about to try calming her, but what would be the point? She obviously knew better than to actually try going after him, which was all that mattered. She had just watched her best friend be murdered for no apparent reason, so anything else she did that didn't put her in danger, she had a right to it.

The truth of what had just happened was finally starting to dawn on him. Cory was a murderer. He wasn't just the whiny asshole that everyone had assumed he was, but was, in fact, a full-blown psychopath. In fact, now that Simon thought about it, Cory was also probably the reason for the disappearance of Lucas.

Miriam seemed to come to this conclusion at roughly the same time as Simon. "Oh my God," she said as she put her hands to her mouth. "I can't believe this is happening. He's a murderer. He's really a…" She spun around and looked in the direction of where she had last seen Katherine, as though she might be able to do something for her now that Cory was out of the way. But the spot in the water where she had disappeared was now calm and completely free of sharks. If there had been any further gruesome display like what had happened with Lara, they had both missed it during their tussle with Cory.

So it was official now. Only three of them remained, and it seemed likely that one of them wanted the other two dead.

# CHAPTER THIRTEEN

"I know I keep asking this, but I just don't understand why. Why did he do this?"

Simon turned his head to look at Miriam. Despite her assertion that she kept asking, this was, in fact, the first thing she had said in about five minutes. After the adrenaline of their fight with Cory wore off, they had both plopped down with their backs against each other in the center of the island and cried in relative silence. That island was still getting smaller, and they still had no clear and safe way off of it, but for these few minutes, neither of them could do anything. Any shock they had felt earlier was nothing compared to what both of them felt now.

"I don't know," Simon finally answered. "He must have had some kind of twisted reason. Maybe he thought he could survive better if he didn't have to worry about anyone else. One thing I'm pretty sure of, though: it came too easy to him. I'm willing to bet that he's done it before. Everything he told me about his past was probably a bullshit lie to cover up whatever horrible things he's done and the real reason he was on this trip."

"Great," Miriam said. "Out of all the tours Katherine and I could have possibly gone on, we had to end up on the one that had a murderer hiding out on it."

The two of them were sitting back to back, trying to give each other both support and warmth. Miriam shivered uncontrollably, but Simon didn't think that was all from just the cold rain. Carefully, so as not to disturb or startle her, he turned himself so that he could put his arms around her. Maybe that would both give her comfort and keep her warm. He would have put Katherine's poncho on her, but somehow during the struggle with Cory, the poncho had gone missing, likely accidentally kicked into the water to flow down the river and never be seen again. For whatever reason she was shivering, it subsided when he had his arms around her.

"Sorry I'm having a freak-out," she said.

"Why would you be sorry? I think you're entitled to one at this point."

"You're not having one."

"For all I know, I will later. And I wasn't the one who just watched my friend get murdered. If anything, I'm a little concerned that you're even as calm as you are."

"Shock, I guess."

"You and Katherine seemed pretty close."

"We've been friends since middle school, although we had our ups and downs. I guess I wasn't always the best friend to her. I stole her boyfriend once."

Simon had to turn to look at her as she said this, as it almost sounded like she announced this fact with a smile. True enough, there was a smirk on her face.

"From your expression, I almost want to say you're joking."

"Yeah, I didn't really. She had a picture she'd surreptitiously taken of a boy she liked. I thought it was unhealthy for her to be obsessing over him like that and I took it, so we've joked around about it ever since that I stole her boyfriend." Her smile suddenly disappeared. "The funny thing is, I always did kind of feel guilty about it, as silly as it was. I always almost wanted to apologize. Now I guess I won't be able to."

Something in her tone suggested she suddenly wanted a moment of quiet with her own thoughts, so Simon stood up. As he did so, he saw that the sharks were once more back to swimming languidly around their island rather than Cory's.

Simon moved as close to the water as he felt comfortable with, hoping to get a better look at the ravenous creatures that had been making their lives hell all night long. Despite the rains, the water was incredibly clear, allowing him a view of the portion of the sharks below the surface. Unfortunately, bull sharks had not been among the various bits of wildlife he had made an effort to study before this trip, so he had no idea whether these were larger or smaller than normal for their species. Even with the night-lit waters keeping him from seeing too much, though, he could tell that each bull shark was at least longer than he was tall. None of the three living tourists, not even the fittest among them (which was unfortunately Cory) would have been able to fight off these beasts while in the water with them.

"I never even realized there *were* sharks in the Amazon River," Miriam said quietly beside him. "Even when you mentioned it earlier, I figured it had to be bullshit. You know, something you were making up to try to get in my pants."

"Uh, is that typically a way that guys try to get in your pants?" Simon asked. Despite the situation, he couldn't help but chuckle a little bit. "By telling you lies about sharks and pink dolphins?"

"No, of course not, but you obviously weren't a typical guy. I mean, you were enjoying standing out in the rain, for Christ's sakes." She cocked her head, and she even smiled a little. "You were trying to seduce me, right? I wasn't misreading those signals?"

"I was actually under the impression that you were the one trying to seduce me," Simon said. "But I certainly wasn't complaining."

The brief moment of levity they had built between them collapsed, and Miriam turned back to stare with haunted eyes back at the circling monsters in the water. "We're really not going to survive this, are we?"

The best thing to do for morale probably would have been to disagree with her, but after everything he'd seen so far since getting on that damned boat, he couldn't manage the energy to be positive. "I suppose there's a chance we could, but I don't see it as likely. That doesn't mean I'm planning on giving up, but I do think we should be prepared for the worst-case scenario."

Miriam made a humorless snort. "Aren't we already in the middle of the worst-case scenario?"

Simon couldn't help but smile, even though there was absolutely nothing funny here. "I suppose so. I guess I meant it as a figure of speech. We're going to need to get ready, though, and go with our original plan. Once the island is underwater, we're not going to have any other option but to swim for it."

"Maybe there's something we can do to give ourselves a better chance," Miriam said.

Simon looked at the pieces of his erstwhile raft. The knots they had used had come undone, but that didn't mean they couldn't try putting it together again. The hoped-for supplies he'd wanted from the boat had never ended up in his hands, so he was limited in what he could do to repair it. Still, there had been that duffel bag. It occurred to him suddenly that he'd never even had the chance to mention it to Miriam, given the chaos that had come immediately after he had seen it, but he rectified that and told her now. She looked thoughtful about it, but ultimately shook her head.

"If you can get the raft back together and get another long enough piece of driftwood to act as a guiding pole, then maybe. But I saw how the pole you have to push you along was already dangerously short. It was barely enough to push you along before, so it definitely won't work now."

"We should get the raft back into shape immediately then," Simon said. "It might just be me, but I think the water might be rising faster right now. If I had to guess, I'd say we have less than an hour to go."

"Right," Miriam said, although there was no enthusiasm behind her words. The raft was still sitting at the edge of the water where Simon had left it, but in their neglect, the thing was dangerously close to floating away. Simon snatched it up, although in his exhausted state, he found that even this simple act was difficult. He hadn't eaten, he'd barely slept, and his muscles were still sore from the unique upper-body workout of using a pole to push the raft against the flow of the Amazon. As he backed away from the water, he saw one of the shark fins react and head in his direction, only for it to turn around when it got too close to the shore. There was something almost lazy about its movements, as though it knew there was no hurry and that these final two tasty morsels would be in the river with it shortly. All it had to do was wait and it would get a yummy snack.

As Cory put the raft in the center of the island again for them both to work on, he said, "If we actually had time for it, I wish we could study the way the bull sharks are acting. I don't know a lot about bull sharks specifically, but so much about their behavior seems out of the ordinary."

"Which parts of their behavior?" Miriam asked as she too got to work.

"Well, for one, and forgive me for bringing it up, but there seem to be five sharks that have eaten three full humans at this point. It just seems to be that they shouldn't be attacking us anymore. Shouldn't they be full? And the other thing is how close they get to the shore. They're almost close enough to beach themselves most of the time. I mean, they're not small animals, so the shallow parts should practically be stranding them and getting them stuck. Yet they don't seem to care."

"Maybe there's a really good reason for it," Miriam said. "Maybe they're not actually normal bull sharks. Maybe they're hungrier than we thought. Maybe you don't really know that much about sharks. Maybe they were genetically engineered by Dr. Evil as killing machines and he just forgot to put the fricking laser beams on their heads this morning. None of that really matter right now, does it? All we need to know is that there are sharks, they can kill us, and they don't seem to want to stop. So maybe turn off your brain for five seconds and instead concentrate on helping me help us survive."

Simon blinked at her admonishment, but she was right. The *whys* of their situation weren't important just now. Should they ever make it back out of the Amazon rainforest and back to somewhere where he could comfortably contemplate anything, then he could question why a shark might not act exactly the way he thought it should. But all that needed to wait for later.

For now, there was just him and Miriam, and a badly made raft, and an island that was visibly shrinking with every second and leaving them closer to their own deaths.

# CHAPTER FOURTEEN

Simon's pounding heart was a steady drumbeat in his ears as he worked frantically on the raft, watching his hands do the work with one eye while the other he kept on the nearby water level. What had been a decent-sized patch of land when they'd first abandoned the boat was now roughly six feet in diameter, and receding fast. He could actually see the minute shrinking of the island from all sides now, and the patch of muddy land on which he and Miriam stood was becoming increasingly cramped.

"Is that it?" Miriam asked, pulling her hands back from the completed raft, although "completed" might not have been the best word for it. They hadn't been able to salvage all of the pieces that Simon had used the first time, so the raft, already small enough that its usefulness had been questionable, was even more reduced in size. The only plus-side to this was that their piddly excuse for a rope, with fewer pieces of wood and debris to hold together, had been tied tighter and wrapped around more pieces this time.

"That's all we can do with it," Simon said. The six feet around them had become four feet. "We're going to have to work with what we have and just go."

"Fine," Miriam said. "So let's grab the…" She paused and looked around them. There wasn't a lot of room left for her to move without stepping in the water. "Wait, where'd it go?"

"Where'd what go?" Simon asked.

"The pole! The one you were using to push yourself along while you were on the raft. It was right next to me, and now it's gone!"

A quick look around their feet confirmed that she was correct. Simon looked up just in time to see the branch that he'd used for a pole as it floated out into the early-morning darkness on the river. While they'd been frantically trying to finish the raft, the water had quietly snuck up on them and stolen the only way they could actually make the raft work to their advantage. Without it, the raft was nearly useless.

Nevertheless, Simon picked up the raft. "We'll just have to try to make do without it."

"It'll never work," Miriam said.

Simon was about to tell her that she shouldn't be so negative, but he surprised himself by saying out loud exactly the opposite. "You're right. Trying to get to shore on the raft isn't going to work like this."

Even as he said it, Simon felt the water come through his ruined sneakers and again bite his toes with its iciness. Their patch of land was officially gone. It was only a matter of minutes before the water would be deep enough for the sharks to start harrying them, and soon after, they probably wouldn't be able to stand anymore.

"We have to swim," Simon said to Miriam.

"Swim where?" she yelled in a slightly manic tone. Honestly, it was surprising that she was as in control of herself as she was. Simon felt like he was only holding onto his own control by the barest thread. "There's nowhere close enough for us to reach before the sharks get us."

"No, there is a place," he said. "But neither of us are going to like it."

At the same time, they both turned to look over at the only other visible patch of land that seemed to be in swimming distance. Cory sat on his own island further down and deeper out on the river, but he was staring at them with added interest now that the two of them seemed to be in danger. Or at least Simon thought that was how he looked. Even after all this time of letting his eyes adjust, it was still hard for Simon to see that far and be certain. The one thing they knew for sure was that the murderer's shape was out there, standing on a patch of land that had not yet reached the same dire situation as their own. He could see the presumably dead body of the deckhand, though, still sprawled out in the mud exactly where they had seen him collapse. It made the island an even less desirable destination, but it was the only choice they had. And they wouldn't just be swimming, Simon realized. They still had the raft, and while it probably wouldn't make any more major journeys, it still might be useful in this situation.

"I've got an idea, but we don't have time to talk about it," Simon said. "We just have to start moving, and if we make it there, the idea worked. If we don't, we'll be too dead to discuss it anyway."

"I'm going to trust you," Miriam said. The water started to cover their feet as Simon grabbed hold of the raft. "Don't make me regret it."

There was no more time to add that she wouldn't have the chance to regret it if they didn't make it.

Simon held the raft in one hand and Miriam's hand in the other. "Go!" he cried. The two of them dashed through the shallow water, quickly finding it too deep to run through and then having to begin their swimming instead. Simon let go of her hand, but kept the raft in his other. The way he was carrying it, the makeshift contraption hindered his swimming speed, but he wouldn't let it go.

And it was a good thing he didn't, either, since as soon as they were both in the water and fighting the pull of the river to get to the next island, the sharks' fins started to pop up in the water again.

"Faster!" Simon tried to call, but it wasn't something that came out coherent, considering all the water threatening to go down his throat. Miriam was a smaller target for the sharks, so hopefully, they wouldn't go for her first, but Simon made sure to splash more and generally make himself more appealing as prey. The actions seemed to work, as the fins came for him instead of her.

*I hope this works*, Simon thought. His swimming mostly came to a stop as he gripped the raft at either side and held it up as well as he could in the water, forming a flimsy shield between him and the charging sharks. One hit him, and several of the branches and pieces of wood bowed dangerously without quite breaking. He kept moving, although he fell significantly behind Miriam, while the sharks circled around him to try to take him from another angle.

*Oh shit. This was definitely not the best idea*, Simon thought as he desperately flailed to get the raft/shield onto his other side before the sharks came at him again. He got it into position just in time to feel something huge and heavy slam against it. This time, the wood did more than bow. Multiple pieces snapped in half right down the middle, effectively turning the raft into little more than a series of broken shards tied together with string. While he knew he might be better off letting go of it altogether in order to maximize his swimming speed, some instinct told him to hold on.

If he survived this, every bit of material he could hold might come in handy, included sodden rope and broken wood.

Given the failure of their two previous attacks, the sharks seemed to decide that they might be better off going after something different for prey. Miriam had significantly pulled ahead of him in her strokes, but that still didn't put her completely out of the range of the sharks. Several of the fins vanished below the water, which to Simon implied that they were going to do the same trick from earlier in the night and swim up at her from directly below.

"Miruuuummmmmm!" Simon called, her name getting cut off as he accidentally swallowed what felt like a gallon of river water once he opened his mouth. He spat it out, put his head as far up above the water as he could, and then tried again. "Miriam, they're going to come up from below you!"

Miriam made a quick motion that almost looked like a nod, then did something that Simon himself would have never considered. Instead of trying to outswim or dodge her attackers, Miriam dove directly down below the surface and out of sight. Simon had no clue what this might accomplish, nor did he have the time or the ability to try coming to her assistance. Instead, he forced himself to take several deep breaths of precious air, then pushed forward toward Cory's island with all his might.

A part of his brain had never expected him to actually make it, so he was shocked into almost swallowing another mouthful of water when he found his hands and knees touching the muddy river bottom at the edge of Cory's island. While he knew he should worry about himself first and pull himself all the way up onto the (relatively speaking) dry land, he couldn't help but turn once he could stand in order to see what had become of Miriam. He was almost convinced that he would see yet another bloody patch rising up out of the water, but at first, he didn't see anything at all. Then, after a few seconds, the water churned and Miriam erupted to the surface like she had dived down deep and then come up with the speed of a rocket. She was only a few feet away from Simon, close enough that he could reach out his hands to assist her and pull her closer to the shore.

As they stumbled up onto land and then collapsed to their knees, Simon saw several fins appear where Miriam had just been. The sharks, apparently, were going to have to go hungry again for just a little longer.

Simon couldn't help himself. He held up the hand that wasn't still holding the remains of the raft and extended his middle finger to the sharks. For obvious reasons, the sharks didn't react, but for just that tiny moment, that small act of rebellion against nature made him feel a little better.

# CHAPTER FIFTEEN

For a moment, with both Simon and Miriam sitting there on their knees in the mud, Simon was certain that Cory would do something to force them back into the river. The man had already shown himself to be absolutely bugshit nuts, and there was no reason for him to be any different now. Instead, however, the man simply sat there in his own patch of mud, looking thoroughly miserable in the rain.

"Are you going to try anything on us?" Miriam asked him.

He looked at her through a matted curtain of his black hair. "Would you even believe me if I said that I wouldn't?"

"No," Miriam admitted. "Psychos like you lie about that kind of stuff just on instinct."

Cory shrugged. "Then I don't see any good reason to tell you whether I plan to or not." He then lay back in the mud and pulled his ragged piece of clothing over his face like he intended to sleep. Simon kept staring at him, half expecting him to leap up at any second and try to kill them, but the murderer did, in fact, seem to be tired. Apparently, killing his boat mates and then swimming for another small island was an exhausting day's work.

For one brief, horrible moment, Simon considered attacking Cory while his guard was down, then doing to Cory exactly what he had done to Katherine and presumably Lucas. He had no doubt that Cory would show his psychopathic tendencies again, and the smart thing to do might have been taking the bastard out before that could happen. A part of him insisted that such an act would make him just as bad as Cory, while another part told him it would just be pre-emptive self-defense. The first part won out, at least for now, but Simon knew a moment might come in the future where he and Miriam might be forced to do something they didn't want to in order to remain safe from the bastard.

Since Cory seemed content to let them be for the moment, however, Simon instead let his attention go to their new island. At the beginning of the night, it probably would have seemed more than large enough to keep the flood waters at bay. Now, however, it was slightly smaller than the other island had been when they first ended up on it. It did rise a little bit higher in the middle than the first, though, so it would probably take longer for this one to completely vanish under the water like the last one. It was hardly safe, but it was better than where they had been.

The only other noticeable feature of their new island was, of course, the dead and limp body of the deckhand lying on its side in the middle of everything. While Miriam kept an eye on Cory, Simon knelt down next to the man and tried to determine what exactly he had died from. The dark sticky substance of his blood had been mostly washed away by the rain, but there was still enough that Simon was confident he had bled out from one of the multiple wounds evident on his body. Several of them looked like bite marks. Apparently, while the tourists had been unmolested by the sharks in their initial swim to the island, the same could not be said of the deckhand. His eyes were both still open, so Simon stooped down next to the body to close them, then stepped away and kept his distance.

"Okay, so now what?" Miriam asked.

Simon felt an unreasonable anger rising up inside him, and it took every ounce of self-control within him to not just scream out that he didn't know. He was not a leader, and never had been. He didn't consider himself a follower either, but rather preferred to keep to himself. Yet here he was, being forced into the position for the hundredth time that night, and he didn't have the mental energy anymore to keep up with it.

"How the hell should I know?" Simon said, his voice raised higher than the calm sentence he had intended. "Why does everyone even keep turning to me for this shit?"

"Because if I don't, I'd have to turn to him," Miriam said, nodding her head in Cory's direction. Cory responded to her by half-heartedly raising a middle finger at her.

"And you can't be the so-called leader here?" Simon asked her. "You sure as hell seem capable enough."

"Why is everyone obsessed with who's the leader and who isn't?" Miriam asked. "There is no leader. It's just a bunch of people trying to survive together. Despite all your insistence that you can't be the leader, you were still the one taking the initiative before everyone else. So we've been treating you like it. If you'd rather not be, just sit the hell down in the mud and act sorry for yourself for a while as everyone else does the work. Otherwise, let's all shut up about who's in charge and just work the damned problem."

Stunned into silence, Simon just sat there as Miriam took the pathetic remains of their raft and began to inspect it. Despite her admonishment, though, none of them actually seemed to be working on their problem. Miriam, using the raft as her excuse to be alone, broke down into silent tears away from the other two. That left Simon with Cory, who might have accepted a temporary truce again, but still had a question that he needed to answer.

"Why?" Simon said to Cory. "No bullshit this time. Just tell me why you killed Lucas and Katherine. I'll know if you're lying."

"You didn't know I was lying before though, did you?"

"Cut the crap and answer me."

Cory shook his head. "Sometimes I don't get people. You're actually standing here asking me why I killed some jackasses you decided you liked. And you obviously think I'm capable of doing it again. So tell me, instead of waffling around and asking why I killed them, why aren't you trying to kill me?"

Simon was taken aback by the question, and yet somehow it felt important to give a truthful, thought-out answer. "Because I'm not a killer. I would never do that."

"You would never *want* to do that, maybe, but are you honestly trying to tell me that if someone was standing over you with an ax raised above their head, and you knew for certain that they were going to kill you because you'd already seen them split open the skulls of several people, and all of a sudden you realized you had a loaded gun in your hand pointed right at the killer's head, you wouldn't fire? It's so important to you that you're not seen as a killer that you would refuse to take another life to defend yourself?"

"Well, no, that's different. In that hypothetical situation, I would pull the trigger. I would kill in self-defense, but never in cold blood."

"And now here I am, Simon, sitting right in front of you," Cory said. "I've killed two people, one of them right before your eyes when you couldn't do anything about it. So I ask you again, why aren't you trying to kill me?"

"Because it wouldn't be self-defense."

"And why wouldn't it be self-defense? Because I'm not

actively in the motion of raising that ax over my head to split open your head and spill your brains all over where the sharks can feast on them? What if I had the ax in hand and was walking toward you? Or I was just picking up the ax? How about if I said I was going to pick up the ax and treat you like a cord of wood out behind the shed? At what point does it become self-defense, and therefore something that's magically okay for you to do?"

Simon was too tired for these mind games, or else he might have been able to give a definitive answer. Instead, he asked, "What does any of this have to do with my original question?"

"If you were half as smart as you thought you were, you would have killed me already to make sure I don't interfere with your survival later," Cory said. "There wouldn't be anything wrong with that. It would be self-defense, as you say."

Finally, Simon realized the insane reasoning he was trying to use with this. "Are you trying to say that hauling off and throwing an innocent young woman into a group of hungry bull sharks somehow counts as self-defense in your book?"

"Self-preservation, at least," Cory said. "I guess you could say I was weeding out the weak ones. Get rid of them now before they have an opportunity to mess things up later and put the real survivors into a position that they can't live through."

Miriam had apparently been listening to this entire conversation, and her tone of voice when she joined in told Simon that she was on the edge of losing her shit over it. "And what about me, huh? You were about to kill me right along with my best friend. You thought my continued existence was a threat to yours?"

Cory nodded, but there was something else to his expression that Simon couldn't identify. Whatever it was, he didn't like it. "That is exactly what I thought, but I see that I was wrong. Very wrong."

Cory turned away from them then as if to signal that he was completely done with this conversation, and no attempt by either of them to engage him again met with any success. After a minute or two, Simon simply decided it was best to leave him alone. He didn't actually want to keep talking to that monster anyway.

# CHAPTER SIXTEEN

Simon had again joined Miriam in attempted repairs on the raft, although neither of them got far in their task before Miriam looked up and, for a moment, almost looked hopeful.

"Wait. Please tell me someone else is noticing that," Miriam said.

Simon almost asked her what she was talking about. At this point, he'd been so focused on their survival that he hadn't even been paying attention anymore to that one environmental hazard that had been causing all this in the first place. But now that Miriam mentioned it, he realized that the rain, that ever-present bane of their current existence, was slowing down significantly. And with the slowing rain, the blackness around them was lightening. Oh, it was still definitely night, but the clouds were thinning, allowing just a tiny hint of moon and starlight through.

And not only that, but the night seemed to be lightening even without the change in weather. They probably had an hour at most left before it became light enough to see well. In general, that might all sound like good fortune for them, but after Simon thought about it, all of this would probably be too little too late.

Miriam held out her hand to cup the falling rain, as if that would prove to her that it was indeed slowing to a drizzle. "If the rain is slowing down or stopping, that means we won't have to worry about the river rising anymore, right?"

"Just because the rain is stopping here doesn't mean the rain is over farther up the river," Simon said. "And it would still rise from the runoff coming off the land. So no, our island is still going to shrink."

"But we can still use this to our advantage, right?" Miriam asked. "I mean, at the very least, visibility is going to be better. And with the sun coming up, we might be able to make the shore."

"Maybe," Cory said. "But probably only if one of us acts as shark bait to lure away the bull sharks while the other two get away."

"No one is going to be shark bait," Simon said. He looked now to both the north and south, hoping that the increased light could now give them an idea of exactly how far they were from either shore. And indeed, he could now see the darkened silhouettes of trees against the slowly lightening sky in both directions, finally allowing him some sense of their place in the river. The south bank of the river was closer, but unfortunately, it would have been even closer still if they had tried to go for it while they were on the other island. If only…

"Shark bait," Miriam suddenly said. "Shark bait!"

Simon gave her a confused look. "I really hope you're not volunteering."

"I don't have to volunteer," Miriam said. "None of us do. Don't you guys see what is literally right in front of us? We already have a volunteer, or at the very least someone who isn't in any position to say no."

Simon blinked. Now that he thought about it, it was a simple solution they should have thought of before, but they hadn't been in the right mindset for it. After all, they hadn't been desperate enough to consider the dead deckhand as anything more than a tragic victim. Now, though, they had no choice but to look at the dead body and see it for the tool it could now be.

Of course, for just a second, he recoiled at the idea of disposing of the deckhand's body in such a callous, thoughtless way. But only for a second. If trapped soccer teams in the Andes could resort to cannibalism of their dead teammates in order to survive, then using the deckhand as a lure for the sharks seemed tame by comparison.

Simon didn't bother to ask Cory what he thought of the plan. He was sure that the young man lacked the same scruples about such a thing. "Okay, so we can use the deckhand's body to distract the sharks. That's one thing we may not have to worry about, but what about the others?"

"Let's list all our concerns out and address them one by one," Simon said. "The worst, of course, is the sharks, but hopefully our bait will keep them away from us. The second is the distance and whether or not we'll be able to swim that far with as tired as we all are." There was enough light now that they all could make out the southern shore. It confirmed what he'd suspected earlier, that the retreat to the second island had actually put them farther away from the relative safety of the land rather than helping them. The boat, on the other hand, was closer. The river didn't seem to be moving as fast now that the rain had slowed almost to a stop, or maybe that was just Simon's imagination, but the boat still looked like it could act as a halfway point between the island and the shore. "We can go to the boat first, hopefully even putting some distance between us and the sharks before they finish with their snack. We could even grab the duffel bag on the way from there to the shore."

Miriam looked in the direction of the boat with a frown. "You know, I absolutely believe that you saw it there, but even with the darkness starting to go away, I don't see it myself."

Simon went to her side so he could point it out, but for several horrifying seconds, he thought it was completely gone. Then he saw it, although that didn't make him feel any better. The duffel bag was indeed no longer where he had initially seen it stuck in the ruined railing of the boat, which was actually a good thing, as that portion of the railing had been submerged in the rising waters. What wasn't so good was that the handles of the duffle bag had gotten caught on what looked like a portion of a fallen tree or an exposed root that was poking out of the water nearby the boat. It bobbed in the water, and although it didn't look like it was going anywhere just yet, the branch it was caught on looked strained as the bag was pulled with the current. That duffel bag wouldn't be there much longer, and once that branch broke, the bag and any useful, life-saving survival items that might be inside would be lost forever to the perpetual flow of the Amazon River.

Simon pointed out its new location to Miriam and Cory. "Shit," Simon said. "If we don't find a way to get it immediately, we can kiss it goodbye."

"And how exactly do you propose to do that?" Cory asked. "You sure as hell can't swim out to it."

Simon thought of the rope he'd used to tie the raft together. It wasn't particularly strong, and it had already gone through a lot throughout the night, but when he thought about its length, he thought it might just be enough.

"Actually, that's exactly what I plan on doing," Simon said.

"Please tell me there's more to your plan than just that," Miriam said.

"There is, but unfortunately not a lot. We'll need to find a couple of rocks first. Big ones, heavy ones, but not so heavy that you and Cory can't throw them."

"We may not have much of anything on this island," Cory said, "but we do have lots and lots of rocks." He indicated the center of the island where the rocky portion provided both the highest point as well as the deckhand's current resting place. There were a number of large, smooth rocks here, ranging from the size of a pebble to the size of a football.

"Both of you grab a whole bunch. Cory, you take the heavy ones. You'll be throwing them at the far side of the island, as far away from the duffle bag as possible. Wait until the sharks circle over to that area, then start lobbing. If we're lucky, you'll bean a few and knock them senseless. That would give me one or two less bull sharks to worry about. But the real important thing is just to keep their attention away from me. Make it seem like some new prey is over there splashing around. Maybe rub some of the deckhand's blood on the stones in order to get their scent up."

"And just what exactly would I be doing during all this time?" Miriam asked.

Simon smiled grimly. "You, Miriam, are going to have to show me whether or not you throw like a girl."

Miriam frowned at what she presumed was an insult, then smiled and nodded as she realized what he wanted from her.

# CHAPTER SEVENTEEN

"Okay. Are we ready?" Simon asked.

"About as ready as we're going to get," Miriam said. "This is your last chance to try pulling out of this crazy plan."

She was right. It was crazy. There was a very good chance that he was about to die all because of a duffel bag that, for all they knew, might only contain someone's underwear. And yet Simon still wanted to do this. Maybe his sense of what was important had been warped over the course of the long night on their little river islands, but he wanted a win here, and that duffel bag represented one to him.

"Just make sure you hold onto that rope," Simon said. "Even if I get to the end of it and the bag is still out of reach, don't let go."

Miriam nodded. The rope that had previously been used to keep their pathetic raft tied together was now in one of her hands, with the other end going to a loop around one of his ankles. The rope was definitely not going to be long enough to reach the duffel, which was where the rock in her other hand came in.

"Get your ass moving already," Cory said. He had his own pile of much larger stones at the ready, some in his hands and some at his feet. Before Simon could respond to him, Cory took one particularly heavy stone and lobbed it as far as he could from the island in the opposite direction of Simon. Simon waited only long enough to see a couple of the fins headed to investigate the sound, then waded out into the water and started swimming.

Adjusting his angle in order to fight against the river's flow, Simon didn't head directly in the direction of the bag. Instead, he tried to get himself at a more or less stationary point in the water just downstream from it. He felt the rope go taut at his angle, signaling that this was as far as he could safely go.

Now was the point where everything could go terribly wrong.

From the other end of the island, Simon could hear Cory continuing to lob his bloody rocks into the water and making a general commotion, but there was no guarantee that would be enough to keep the sharks away from him. And Miriam's aim with her own rocks would need to be precise. It suddenly occurred to Simon that if she missed her target by too much, the rocks she threw might bean him instead, and he would probably be knocked unconscious and drown before he could do anything. That would certainly be an embarrassing way to go after everything they had already survived, but at least it would come with the small comfort that the only witnesses to his humiliating death would likely die themselves before they could report to the world what had happened to him.

Simon tried to call out to Miriam that now was the time to throw, but all he could manage was a sputter as he tried to raise his head over the water long enough to talk. Miriam understood anyway and launched her first stone. She was a good throw, but her target was rather small. The rock easily sailed over and past Simon toward the branch where the duffel was caught, but it missed the target and plopped into the water nearby.

"Sorry!" Miriam called out. Again, any attempt Simon made to tell her it was fine simply turned into him gargling river water. She grunted as she hurled another one. This rock came closer, being only inches away from the bag, but it still didn't dislodge it.

Simon swam in place against the current for several more seconds, waiting for her to try again, but nothing came. He turned his head just enough to something moving in the water closer to the island. At the same time, Miriam called out to him.

"Simon, the sharks stopped going after Cory's decoy rocks! They're coming after you now!" She looked like she was about to start yanking on the rope.

"No, not..." He actually managed two whole words this time before he swallowed more water. Instead, he frantically gestured at the bag, hoping Miriam would take that to mean that she should try one more time before pulling him in. He kept an eye out around him the whole time, realizing that all five fins were now visible and heading his way.

There was a horrible moment of pause, then another grunt of exertion as Miriam made her last attempt. The rock sailed over him and hit the branch, snapping it and allowing the bag to float with the current toward him. It was almost too far away and threatened to slip through his fingers, but he got a grip on it at the last possible second before it floated out of range to disappear down the Amazon.

"Got it!" Simon screamed. "Pull me back! Pull me back!"

The two dorsal fins nearest him abruptly changed direction, heading straight for him. At the same time, Simon felt an uncomfortable jerk on the rope around his ankle. The fiber bit into the skin just above his sock, and only now did he realize that it might be rubbing his skin raw and putting blood in the water that might be whipping the sharks into even more of a frenzy. Unthinkingly, he tried to turn his head to look if there were any of the bull sharks somewhere behind him, closer to the source of the flowing blood, and he got a mouthful of river water for his floundering efforts.

One of the sharks dashed directly at him, only to miss as one particularly sharp tug on the rope yanked him back another couple feet. The canvas strap on the duffel bag almost slipped out of his fingers as he was pulled away, but he got an iron grip on it just in time to keep from losing it in the flow of the river. Another shark came close to snapping at him just as he sensed that the water beneath him was shallow enough that he could stand. Remembering how Katherine had died even in shallow water where the sharks shouldn't have been able to follow, Simon wasted no time splashing his way back to relatively dry land. Even while he'd been gone, the land had continued to vanish underneath the rising water, but with what he now had in hand, maybe they might actually have a chance to escape before the island disappeared completely.

Simon took only a few seconds to catch his breath once he was back on land before he yanked open the zipper of the duffle back to see what might be inside. Both Cory and Miriam stood over him, trying to get a glimpse of the contents.

"Well?" Cory asked. "Anything we can use in there?"

"The bag itself seems to be watertight enough to be filled with air and used as a flotation device, so if nothing else, we have that," Simon said. "As far as the contents…"

He upended the bag and dumped what was inside onto the wet ground. When he'd first seen it, he'd thought it was one of the bags that the tourists had brought with them and wouldn't include anything more than clothes. It did have a few shirts and socks in it, but it must have belonged to either the captain or one of the deckhands, as it had a few pieces of useful survival gear as well. There was a small first-aid kit that included antibiotic ointment, several bandages, over-the-counter painkillers, and a few other less useful items like band-aids. There was also a Swiss army knife and a compass. None of that stuff was particularly useful for them in this particular moment, but if they did get off the island, then they could definitely help in the next phase where they had to survive long enough to reach civilization.

"This is good," Simon said. "We can use these." But none of it, he felt, was as useful or important as the last item he found. There was a rope, and not just the thin, weak one they'd been forced to use to keep the raft together and to tie around his ankle. This one was thick, new nylon, and when it was unraveled, it appeared to be at least twenty feet in length. Simon held it up for the other two to see.

"We can use this to hold together the raft," Simon said. "With it and the other rope, we can make it strong enough to hold more than just one of us."

Cory stared at it with an intensity that Simon didn't like. "Yeah, maybe we can, if we can find enough driftwood to replace the parts that broke off when you fought off the sharks."

Simon couldn't quite remember if this was the first agreeable thing Cory had said since they'd met yesterday, but whether it was or not, it made Simon suspicious. Duplicitous, murderous bastards didn't just suddenly become helpful if they didn't see an angle to it. He was planning something, and both Simon and Miriam needed to be on their toes for the moment when he went for it.

"There's a few pieces over here," Miriam said. "Actual pieces of wooden planks. The river must still be washing over broken parts of the boat."

Simon went over to where she was indicating, and sure enough, there were additional bits of the boat that had washed up on their patch of land while they hadn't been paying attention.

Also, now that it was lighter, they could see that this particular island was in a better position relative to the wreck of the boat, where things that had floated down from the wreck were more likely to get caught here than on the other island. There were several good, larger planks of lumber as well as some bigger chunks of driftwood. He nodded as he looked at them, already arranging them in his head into a far sturdier raft than the one he'd been able to concoct before.

"We can do this," Simon said. He looked around at their island, taking careful note of its current size and the rate at which the water was currently rising. "And this time around, I think we can even take the time to give it the care it really needs."

# CHAPTER EIGHTEEN

The raft was done, and they'd even had a length of rope to spare. The duffel bag with their remaining equipment was packed. All that remained was for Cory to prep the deckhand's dead body to be used as a lure to get rid of the sharks, and they would be ready to go.

Even so, Simon felt the need to be cautious. While Cory finished his grim job, Simon pulled Miriam as far away from him as they could go so they could have a moment of privacy.

"Just remember," Simon said to her. "Under no circumstances, no matter what happens or what he says, don't trust him."

"What, you really thought that I would?" Miriam asked. "I've known pieces of shit like him before. Always think they're something special without having earned any such title. I took care of them, and I'm going to take care of him, too. He killed my best friend, remember?"

Yes, Simon definitely remembered, and yet his brain was playing tricks on him, making him feel like Cory's horrifying display with Katherine was much further away in time than it really was. He suspected this was some kind of symptom of shock, and once this was all over, if it actually would be all over at some point for them, he would have a raging case of PTSD to deal with.

Somehow, he doubted that was what Aunt Annie wanted for him when she'd set up this trip.

"I'm sorry," Simon said. "I didn't mean to trivialize that."

"Yeah, that's fine," she said absently. Her tone suggested that she hadn't even heard him, and the faraway look in her eye suggested she was thinking of something else entirely. "So, here's the deal. If we survive this and get to dry land, we can have sex, if you still want."

If Simon had been drinking water, he would have done a spit take.

"But after this is all over, if we get back to civilization, I don't ever want to see you again."

Under other circumstances, Simon might have objected. But he thought he understood Miriam's current state of mind, and truthfully, his own wasn't far from it. His mind had been in survival mode all night, and he thought he had read somewhere how these kinds of extreme circumstances could trigger an intense sensual response, like the body was aware how close it had come to dying and was trying to procreate in response. But even more so, Simon understood her desire to avoid him forever in the future. Simon himself suspected that see her at any point after this would bring back the bad memories, of which he was sure they were still going to make more of.

"I supposed we'll talk about that more if or when we get to shore," Simon said. "In the meantime..." He pulled away from Miriam's side so that Cory could now hear him as well. "Is the body prepared?"

Cory stood up from his work with the Swiss army knife still in hand. The blade was now covered in the clotted blood of the dead deckhand, and Simon couldn't help but notice that the expression on Cory's face was a little too gleeful for comfort. "That should do it," Cory said. "His guts are in enough pieces that they should attract all the sharks well away from us."

"Fine," Simon said. "Now can I have that knife back?"

Cory hesitated, and Simon thought for a moment that Miriam was right and they were about to have a serious problem on their hands. Then Cory flipped the bloody knife in his hand so he was holding the crimson-stained blade and held out the handle for Simon to take. Simon took it, folded away the blade, and then stashed it in one of his pockets.

"So that's everything, right?" Miriam asked. "We're ready to do this?"

There was an interesting quality to Miriam's voice. "You almost sound hesitant," Simon said.

Miriam threw a quick look in the direction of Cory, which Simon interpreted as her saying that she didn't want to talk about it in front of him. Maybe she didn't want to sound weak in front of him or admit she was scared, or maybe it was more that she actually thought he could do something against her if he knew what she was thinking.

Simon looked down at the renewed raft, wondering if maybe it would be a better idea to go the first leg of this journey without it. Trying to take it as far as the boat had been difficult before, so it would be even worse now. Maybe, despite the work they'd put into it, they should just abandon the raft altogether.

As he was staring, a thick, meaty *thwack* noise sounded in the air behind him. He spun around, his reflexes already knowing he should be prepared for a fight even before his mind caught up to what was happening, but it wasn't enough to help him. Cory, with one of the unused pieces of driftwood held in his hand like a club, was standing over Miriam where she lay bleeding on the ground. He swung the club at Simon, hitting him directly in the ribcage, painfully forcing all the air out of his lungs. Simon raised his arms to try to ward off any further blow, but Simon tended to be more of a bookworm; he didn't have much of an idea how to handle himself in a fight. All he managed was to get his left arm up in time to prevent Cory from getting him right across the face. That was enough to knock Simon off his balance, and he fell on his side in the mud at the water's edge.

Simon stared up at Cory with vision that was blurry with pain, lack of sleep, and lack of food. Cory stood over him for a second, looking like he wasn't entirely sure what to do next, before smashing the stick down several times on Simon's ribs. Cory must have been lacking in strength by this point too, as the blows, while still painful, were not quite as hard as they should have been. After that, Cory took a moment to go look at Miriam, still on the ground and writhing in pain, but not fully unconscious from his attack. He took the remaining pieces of rope from their building of the raft, and Simon realized it was just enough to tie up Miriam's wrists.

"What...?" Simon managed to say, but he couldn't catch his breath enough to force out any further words.

"You know, I've told you guys a whole lot of lies over the last twenty-four hours, but I've said true things as well," Cory said. "The stuff about my family, obviously a lie, but the stuff about surviving? That was true. And I plain and simply don't think you sticking around is going to help me get out of here. You're a burden on me that I don't need. Her, on the other hand, I can use. She's a real fighter. I can use her, at least for a while. And when she starts being more of a burden than a help, well, she can go out the same way as everyone else."

Miriam was too out of it to struggle much as Cory pulled her onto the new and improved raft. Cory didn't immediately join her, though. Instead, he pulled Simon over to the other side of the island. At first, Simon didn't understand the point until he found himself sticky with the congealed blood of the dead deckhand next to him. That was the point where Simon truly understood what Cory intended to do.

He didn't just want Simon out of his way. He was planning on using Simon as extra insurance against a shark attack. Because if they would be distracted by one bloody dead body, then they would probably be even more interested in an additional body that was still bleeding and squirming.

Simon tried to struggle back to his feet, but before he could, Cory kicked him repeatedly in the stomach, then brought the branch down on him a couple more times.

"Better stop that now," Cory said to himself as he looked at the branch. "I'm still going to need this thing to steer us on the raft. Wouldn't do me any good to break it against someone as worthless as you."

Confident now that Simon had had the fight beaten completely out of him, Cory ignored him for a second while he picked up the deckhand, stumbled under the dead weight for a bit, and then did his best to pitch the body out into the water. Simon couldn't see where the body went from this angle, but he was sure the sharks would be headed right for it.

Cory half-heartedly kicked Simon one more time for good measure, then pushed him the rest of the way into the water. For a moment, Simon didn't have the strength to fight, and he began to float away with the flow of the river and towards his inevitable death at the teeth of the bull sharks.

# CHAPTER NINETEEN

The cold of the water shocked him back to his senses, and Simon realized he likely only had a matter of seconds to do anything before the sharks were on him. Rather than trying to swim back to the island and again face Cory's wrath, Simon made the split-second decision to deliberately swim toward the dead body floating nearby. Several fins were visible above the water, but he also thought he felt something large churning the water below him. He grabbed the body by its torn shirt just as the first of the sharks came at him, and he twisted so that the body was between him and the predator. Two of the sharks immediately started ripping into the deckhand, and absolutely nothing in their manner suggested they would be more interested in Simon than the much easier meal before them.

With at least two of the sharks distracted and more perhaps on their way to it, Simon turned around and, with all the strength he had left, started swimming against the current. He didn't head directly back for the island, however. In those precious few moments where Simon had been dealing with the sharks, Cory had taken the raft and launched, pushing his way in the direction of the halfway point that was the wrecked boat. Miriam was still semi-conscious on the sodden wooden planks, and Cory was too busy trying to deal with the less-than-cooperative raft to realize that his main nemesis was not shark food, or at least not yet. Simon still had a chance to do something.

Even though Cory was struggling with keeping the raft's movements in check, he still had a significant lead that Simon doubted he would be able to make up easily. As Simon swam in that direction, though, he could see that the raft was starting to come apart. Never before had Simon felt so much relief that he didn't know how to properly build and put things together. Cory was most of the way to the boat when pieces started to break off. He slapped Miriam awake, said something to her, then pulled her over the side of the raft with the duffel bag just as the raft wimped apart completely. Rather than trying to climb up over the side of the boat, Cory grabbed Miriam and pulled her under the water. Given that Simon didn't think he would intentionally drown himself, he had to assume that Cory had found some hole in the hull of the boat to go in. That would have to be where he went as well.

There was splashing from behind him as he got to the point where Cory and Miriam had disappeared. Apparently, the sharks were no longer entertained with their easy meal.

Simon took a deep breath, then forced himself to go under after Miriam and Cory. Keeping his eyes open under the water, he saw a trail of bubbles going into one of the lower holes in the side of the boat. Also, twisting his head to the side, he could see three of the bull sharks diving lower with him and heading straight for him. In the light of the rising morning, he could clearly see them flashing through the water. It was the first time he actually regretted that he could see them now. And to make matters worse, the wound on his ankle from the rope earlier must have opened again, as a fresh small cloud of red was rising near his foot.

He couldn't worry about any of that now. If the sharks were going to get them, then likely his death would be quick. He needed to worry now instead about something he might be able to affect, like the fates of Miriam and Cory. Trying to keep his attention on the boat, he thought he saw a spot deeper in the water where a cloud of rising dirt and mud showed that someone or something had recently passed this way, and given that it was right near one of the larger holes in the hull, he hoped that something had been one of his two targets.

He kicked and stroked hard, angling for the hole, and was surprised at the speed with which he reached it. Grabbing the ragged edges of the boat's hole, he yanked himself in with all the force he could muster. The hole was a tight fit, and he further skinned parts of himself on the jagged wood, but the hole's size would also prevent any of the sharks from getting in. Or, at least, they couldn't get in through that hole. If there was another, larger one nearby, he could be in trouble later.

He'd been prepared to have to continue holding his breath for a dangerously long time once he was inside the wreck, but he lucked out within the very first room. He only had to go up about a foot and a half before he entered a trapped pocket of air, and from there, he could take a brief moment to catalog his surroundings. He was below deck in what he suspected was supposed to be the sleeping quarters, although he hadn't really had a chance to go in except to drop off his supplies. Several sodden mattresses floated on the surface, and with them was a wide variety of debris that, under other circumstances, he would have scoured for anything useful. He was probably rushing against time, though. Whatever the hell Cory intended to do with Miriam, he wouldn't just sit around waiting for Simon to show up.

While this likely seemed like the direction he had pulled her under the water, there was no sign of either of them in this particular room. He thought he could hear something nearby, though, something that might have been screaming or calling for help. For the first time, Simon wondered just what exactly Cory intended to do with her. If Cory merely wanted to escape, it would have been easier to just dump her in the river rather than wrestle with her on the raft. He had, in fact, tried to kill her earlier in the night, so it wasn't like he had any compunctions about it.

Of course, there was the obvious possibility of what a psycho might want to do when alone with a young woman, but Simon hoped that wasn't it. And if it was, he hoped Miriam still had enough of that feistiness going on after their long night that she would be able to hold Cory off.

Other than the floating debris, there was nothing of interest here, and there didn't appear to be any exit within the small pocket of air, which meant he would have to dive under again to continue. He took a deep breath then ducked under again, searching for whatever exit Cory and Miriam had taken out of this room. He found the door near the bottom, right across from the hole where he'd come in, and took a moment to note that the sharks could still just barely be seen swimming outside. He came back up for one more breath, then went down and through the door. The darkness here was so absolute that he could only tell where he was by feeling with his hands, but he was pretty sure this was the hall that led to the stairs, which in turn had gone up to the main deck. Most of that would be underwater, too, except for the one part of the bow that had still been visible to them from the island, but the cabin could possibly have the same kind of air pocket that he'd found in the previous room. He didn't have time to give this any more consideration, as his lungs were already burning with the desperate need to breathe. Swimming down the narrow corridor, he found the stairs and followed them up. From here, he could see out a door and into the morning sun that was starting to shine on the water, but he didn't think that was where he needed to go. Cory would have still wanted to use the boat as a swimming halfway point between the island and the shore, but he also would have wanted to get anything else he thought he might need to survive once they made it to the jungle. That meant supplies, many of which he would probably find in the cabin.

Simon moved as quickly as he dared, remembering the beatdown Cory had given him on the island and knowing that it would be easy for the lunatic to do the same thing again if he got the drop on him. About all Simon had going in his favor was that Cory probably thought he was still unconscious on that island, or else had fallen prey to the sharks if he'd tried to follow them. At the top of the steep set of stairs, Simon stopped again, trying to ignore the way his lungs burned and his vision flashed at the edges as he judged the safety of the situation. Nothing immediately struck him as dangerous, so he took the chance and popped his head above the water just long enough to take a breath and quickly survey the scene. Before he pulled himself back under, he heard voices, but they weren't directly in the cabin. They'd gone out onto the exposed portion of the deck, likely for Cory to get a breather and decide exactly what he wanted with Miriam. Simon looked around the cabin for anything he could use as a weapon, but there wasn't much. He was going to have to face this bastard with just his hands.

He swam to the door, which was partly submerged, and saw the steeply inclined bow deck from which they had all been ejected early last night. Other than the extreme angle, there was remarkably little damage to indicate that anything had gone wrong with the boat at all.

Simon stood on the deck, having to hold onto the railing and lean perilously in order not to slip and slide down the wet wood. Miriam, who looked like she had a few fresh bruises growing where Simon had hit her to further subdue her, had her hands tied to the railing. She was awake and seemed lucid, and her eyes strayed briefly to Simon coming through the door before they went back to Cory, likely so Cory wouldn't see her looking in his direction. Cory was looking out over the water in the direction of the shore, which was now easily visible in the morning light. The distance between the boat and the shore wasn't that bad, but all the sharks were once again swarming around it. Whether Cory realized it yet or not, they had all followed Simon and were now cutting off their escape.

Carefully making his way over the slick wooden boards, Simon did his best to sneak up on the murderer and his captive. Cory had the duffel bag in one hand and the Swiss army knife in the other, folded open so the blade was out and pointed in Miriam's general direction. He was thoroughly distracted by the multiple fins just below him in the water, so Simon believed there was a pretty good chance he could sneak up on him and get the knife before he had a chance to whirl around and use it on either him or Miriam. Miriam seemed to realize this too, as she started talking to Cory.

"You're looking pretty screwed now, you bastard," she said. "For all your murderous plans, you're still going to be stuck here."

For a moment, Cory seemed to be honestly worried, but when he replied, there was a cold, calculating tone to his voice. "Maybe. Or maybe I've just found the point where I can use you. After all, distracting the sharks with dead bodies worked for a short time before. There's no reason not to assume that it won't work again."

He took a step toward Miriam, the knife held back like he was about to slash it across her throat. That was when Simon made his move and leaped at him.

Simon grabbed Cory by the arm that was holding the knife, and it immediately slipped out of his fingers and fell toward Miriam. If it had fallen blade-down, then it would have embedded itself in her left leg, but instead, it hit with the handle. She was able to close her knees together and catch it before it hit the deck and slid down the incline into the water, but Simon didn't have the time to try taking it from her and using it against Cory. Cory turned and smashed the duffel bag against Simon's face. There wasn't anything in it that particularly hurt him, but it still caught Simon off guard and almost sent him tumbling. Instead, he grabbed the railing and held on with one hand, while with the other he punched Cory in the gut.

"You're supposed to be—" Cory didn't get a chance to finish his statement, as Simon decked him again and attempted to get the duffel bag out of his grasp. Cory slipped and fell against the railing, smashing the flimsy wooden material and creating a cleared path between the two combatants and the shark-infested waters below. Cory caught himself before he went overboard, however, and instead grabbed Simon, both using him as an anchor as well as finally taking the initiative in the attack.

Out of the corner of his eye, Simon saw Miriam squirming to get the handle of the knife from between her legs to her mouth. There was just enough slack on her ropes that she would probably be able to grab the knife from there with her hands. All Simon had to do was stall.

Cory, who was holding Simon down with his head over the edge of the boat, grinned down at him. "Okay, I have to admit that I wasn't thinking clearly here. I should have made sure that you were completely dead before I threw you in the water."

Behind him, Miriam had the knife clenched between her teeth as she stretched to grab it.

"But I'm not going to make that mistake this time," Cory said. He pushed down harder on Simon, forcing his body inch by inch over the side. Simon kept a hold on the duffel with one hand and gripped the ravaged railing with the other. Cory grabbed him by the throat and squeezed, causing Simon's vision to get darker. It wasn't so dark yet, though, that he couldn't see that Miriam now had the knife firmly in hand and was using it to saw through her bonds.

"I'm going to throw you overboard to the sharks, and then I'm going to do the same thing to her. Because let's face it, she's much more trouble than she's worth."

Simon's vision became nothing more than flashing black and white as his oxygen supply diminished. *Come on, Miriam. Please…*

There was a sudden splash of hot fluid over Simon's face, and suddenly he could breathe again. He looked up to see Miriam standing precariously behind Cory, the knife coming away from his throat as the slash she'd made there pulsed with his blood.

Cory let go of Simon and grasped at his own throat as though he thought he might be able to push the blood back in. The look on his face clearly said that he didn't understand what had just happened, nor would he ever get the chance to understand. With his balance clearly off, Simon shoved Cory off of him at the same time that Miriam pushed him toward the gap in the railing. Cory let go of the bag, leaving it in Simon's hand, and then toppled over the side.

Simon turned around and looked over the edge just in time to see the almost-comical sight of Cory's body landing right on one of the shark fins. When the body went under, the sharks did the same, and the water turned swirling red as the sharks got yet another meal.

# CHAPTER TWENTY

Simon would have loved to take a moment just to breathe, but he knew instantly that they couldn't.

"They're distracted," he said to Miriam. "We have to hop off over the other side and swim for it."

Miriam was obviously just as exhausted as Simon, but she nodded. This would be their last chance to lure the sharks away from them long enough to reach the shore. The sun was bright enough that they could see where they were going, and the distance from the boat to the shore was manageable. It was now or never.

They paused only long enough for Miriam to stow the Swiss army knife in a pocket and Simon to make sure the straps of the duffel were secured high up on his arms so as not to interfere too much with his swimming. Then they both leaped over the railing.

*This is the second time in the last twenty-four hours that I've done this*, Simon thought. One way or the other, it would also be the last time.

This time, the temperature of the water wasn't such a shock to his system, as he'd already spent all night sopping wet. The instant they both went below the surface, they started in the direction of the shore, pushing themselves with every last ounce of strength they could still wring from their bodies.

He knew it was a mistake to look back, but halfway between the boat and the shore, Simon couldn't resist. He looked over his shoulder, hoping the sharks would still be working on Cory on the other side of the boat and hadn't even noticed the two new morsels in the water. His hopes were in vain. Three of the shark's fins were heading straight for them, and for all he knew, the other two might be in the water below.

Simon pinwheeled his limbs furiously, forcing his body to move faster than he had ever thought possible in the past. Miriam did the same, although her lesser weight made it easier for her to propel herself through the water and get ahead of him. He suddenly remembered something he and his friends had joked about when they'd been really into zombies and had each come up with a zombie survival plan: you didn't need to be faster than the zombies, you just needed to be faster than the slowest person in your group. And apparently, between him and Miriam, Simon was not going to be the fastest.

Twin thoughts hit him at the same time: *It's okay, I've lived a good life*, and *No, I don't want to die yet*! He didn't have time to consider which feeling was more true, though, as that was the moment he felt something huge and heavy ram him front behind, smashing directly into his leg. From the instant pain, he suspected that the bull shark, in its effort to tenderize him for later consumption, had broken something in Simon's foot or ankle. Even as the pain hit him, though, he realized he was lucky that the shark hadn't managed to actually get its teeth in him. Hopefully, that would provide him with the few extra seconds he needed to get to safety.

Ahead of him, Miriam reached the shore. As she stumbled up onto dry land, she turned and then immediately pointed behind him. "Watch out!" Simon wasn't in any position to make drastic maneuvers, but her warning was enough to make him pull to one side just as one of the sharked torpedoed right at him. He felt its rough skin scrape against him, and instinctually, Simon reached out in an attempt to grab the creature and prevent it from rounding on him. He expected it to slip through his fingers, yet even in the water, he managed to get a grip and hold on, effectively wrestling the shark in the shallows at the edge of the river.

*Oh shit*, he thought. In this position, he might effectively keep this one shark from digging its teeth into him. But it also left him completely open and vulnerable to the other sharks, and if he dared let go, then this one would quickly round on him and end it. He could feel the silt from the river bottom as it swirled in the muck beneath him, though, which meant he had to be close to the shore. He only had to survive long enough to reach dry land.

"Get closer and I can help!" Miriam yelled. Simon did what he could, wriggling in the water and trying desperately to get even a few inches closer to the shore. Miriam stood at the water's edge, the Swiss army knife in her hand and ready to stab the shark as soon as Simon could bring it closer. He struggled, making some progress, when he felt the water shift near his legs.

"Watch out!" Miriam screamed, but Simon was already twisting, trying to put the squirming shark in between him and the other bull sharks coming for him. With one of the sharks, he succeeded, causing it to ram teeth first into the underbelly of the shark in Simon's hands. With the other, he failed. Simon screamed as he felt a white-hot pain in his leg, the sign of the remaining shark getting a bite in. He shook his leg, hoping the shark didn't have enough of a hold that it would stay clamped on, and felt more of his flesh tearing as he dislodged the creature from his calf.

Miriam, now apparently with enough courage to brave the

water again, waded out just far enough that she could stand over the shark in Simon's hands. With a wordless screech, she plunged the small knife down hard enough that it penetrated the shark's rough skin and sent blood spurting everywhere. She pulled it out and then jabbed it out again, all her anger and fear and frustration from their night's ordeal obviously coming to the surface now. Simon had to let go and pull himself farther up on shore to get out of the way of her flailing and the knife, which was now completely covered in the shark's blood and gore. He felt something large come up and snap at the water behind him, but he was far enough out of the water now that the shark couldn't reach him. Other than the dying shark that had been in his arms as it still weakly chomped at the air, Simon was free and clear.

They had made it. They were finally free of the Amazon River.

Both Simon and Miriam collapsed to their knees at the muddy edge of the water, neither of them having the strength left at the moment to do anything more than pant and thank God that they were alive. Simon, still feeling paranoid about the remaining sharks in the river, pulled himself up even further into the underbrush before turning over and letting himself fall on his back. He almost choked for a second on phlegm and river water. Once his airway was clear, though, he suddenly found himself without any energy at all. Part of that might have been from the frantic swim, but he also suspected that part of it was blood loss. The mud all over his body now, while likely to give him some seriously dangerous infections, had at least stopped the blood flow from his mangled leg for the moment.

He realized there was a good chance he would die from his injuries before he was able to reach safety, but for now, he felt an immense relief that he'd been able to simply live this long. And Miriam was still in relatively good shape. Assuming she found help quick enough, she would definitely live.

He felt a pressure on his chest and opened his drooping eyelids to see Miriam over the top of him. There was a distinct look of worry on her face, yet underneath it there was also the relief that they were alive, at least for the moment. "Simon, you look like absolute shit."

"Not surprising," he said. "I feel like absolute shit."

"You still want to have sex?"

Simon started to laugh, but it just turned into him hacking up more water. Even though most of it ended up on Miriam, she didn't seem to mind. After all, getting coughed on was hardly the worst thing that had happened to her on this trip. "I never thought I'd have to turn that down, but I don't think I'm in any shape for that right now. I guess it's not going to happen."

"Well now, I wouldn't say that," Miriam said. "Maybe I've changed my mind about us getting together once we're back in civilization."

"I really don't think I'm going to make it," Simon said, pulling himself up just enough to indicate his severely mangled leg. "Even if I can somehow manage to walk on that thing long enough to reach help, I'm probably going to die from an infection long before that happens."

Miriam finally took the time to take a closer look at his leg, letting out a hiss once she saw exactly how damaged it was. Even so, though, the look of determination never left her face. "So what? Are you seriously just going to give up now? After everything we've survived just to get to this point?"

No, Simon realized. He wasn't ready to just stop all of a sudden. He realized he wanted to get back home, to see his Aunt Annie, to see if maybe there was any possibility of something more with Miriam. And even if there wasn't, there were still plenty of other things to live for.

Simon struggled into a sitting position. "The boat didn't get that far down the river before it wrecked. If we go back in the direction we came and then somehow get back across the river to the north shore, we might be able to find the dock where we started."

Miriam nodded enthusiastically. "And then the road, which even if it is still far from any town, will at least lead us to other people."

"We can do this," Simon said. "Help me bandage my leg, and then we'll start back."

Their chances, he suddenly realized, weren't all that bad after all. Even if his dream vacation had turned out to be a nightmare, it looked like he would still probably wake up from it.

Opening the duffel bag for supplies, the two of them got to work on fixing him up as best they could.

# CHECK OUT OTHER GREAT DEEP SEA THRILLERS

## SEA RAPTOR
by John J. Rust

From terrorist hunter to monster hunter! Jack Rastun was a decorated U.S. Army Ranger, until an unfortunate incident forced him out of the service. He is soon hired by the Foundation for Undocumented Biological Investigation and given a new mission, to search for cryptids, creatures whose existence has not been proven by mainstream science. Teaming up with the daring and beautiful wildlife photographer Karen Thatcher, they must stop a sea monster's deadly rampage along the Jersey Shore. But that's not the only danger Rastun faces. A group of murderous animal smugglers also want the creature. Rastun must utilize every skill learned from years of fighting, otherwise, his first mission for the FUBI might very well be his last.

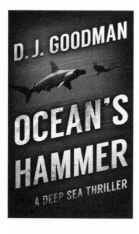

## OCEAN'S HAMMER
by D.J. Goodman

Something strange is happening in the Sea of Cortez. Whales are beaching for no apparent reason and the local hammerhead shark population, previously believed to be fished to extinction, has suddenly reappeared. Marine biologists Maria Quintero and Kevin Hoyt have come to investigate with a television producer in tow, hoping to get footage that will land them a reality TV show. The plan is to have a stand-off against a notorious illegal shark-fishing captain and then go home.

Things are not going according to plan.

There is something new in the waters of the Sea of Cortez. Something smart. Something huge. Something that has its own plans for Quintero and Hoyt.

# CHECK OUT OTHER GREAT
# DEEP SEA THRILLERS

## THEY RISE
## by Hunter Shea

Some call them ghost sharks, the oldest and strangest looking creatures in the sea.

Marine biologist Brad Whitley has studied chimaera fish all his life. He thought he knew everything about them. He was wrong. Warming ocean temperatures free legions of prehistoric chimaera fish from their methane ice suspended animation. Now, in a corner of the Bermuda Triangle, the ocean waters run red. The 400 million year old massive killing machines know no mercy, destroying everything in their path. It will take Whitley, his climatologist ex-wife and the entire US Navy to stop them in the bloodiest battle ever seen on the high seas.

## SERPENTINE
## by Barry Napier

Clarkton Lake is a picturesque vacation spot located in rural Virginia, great for fishing, skiing, and wasting summer days away.

But this summer, something is different. When butchered bodies are discovered in the water and along the muddy banks of Clarkton Lake, what starts out as a typical summer on the lake quickly turns into a nightmare.

This summer, something new lives in the lake...something that was born in the darkest depths of the ocean and accidentally brought to these typically peaceful waters.

It's getting bigger, it's getting smarter...and it's always hungry.

# CHECK OUT OTHER GREAT DEEP SEA THRILLERS

## MEGATOOTH
### by Viktor Zarkov

When the death rate of sperm whales rises dramatically, a well-respected environmental activist puts together a ragtag team to hit the high seas to investigate the matter. They suspect that the deaths are due to poachers and they are all driven by a need for justice.

Elsewhere, an experimental government vessel is enhancing deep sea mining equipment. They see one of these dead whales up close and personal...and are fairly certain that it wasn't poachers that killed it.

Both of these teams are about to discover that poachers are the least of their worries. There is something hunting the whales...

Something big
Something prehistoric.
Something terrifying.
MEGATOOTH!

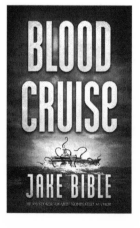

## BLOOD CRUISE
### by Jake Bible

Ben Clow's plans are set. Drop off kids, pick up girlfriend, head to the marina, and hop on best friend's cruiser for a weekend of fun at sea. But Ben's happy plans are about to be changed by a tentacled horror that lurks beneath the waves.

International crime lords! Deep cover black ops agents! A ravenous, bloodsucking monster! A storm of evil and danger conspire to turn Ben Clow's vacation from a fun ocean getaway into a nightmare of a Blood Cruise!

Made in the USA
Middletown, DE
28 August 2019